MW00584387

GUNE
AGAIN

OTHER TITLES BY MINKA KENT

GONE AGAIN

A THRILLER

MINKA KENT

THOMAS & MERCER

Text copyright © 2023 by Nom de Plume, LLC
All rights reserved.

Published by Thomas & Mercer, Seattle

www.apub.com

Amazon, the Amazon logo, and Thomas & Mercer are trademarks of Amazon.com, Inc., or its affiliates.

ISBN-13: 9781662505393 (paperback)
ISBN-13: 9781662505386 (digital)

Cover design by Shasti O'Leary Soudant

Cover images: © Ruben Mario Ramos, © Alexandre Rotenberg / Arcangel Images

Printed in the United States of America

For Milo

CHAPTER 1

CELIA

Twenty-five years ago

"And just like *that*." My father releases a white-knuckled grip from the steering wheel of our rambling family Ford and snaps his fingers. "We'll be driving down the road, and suddenly the three of us will be gone, Celia. Your mother. Your sister. Me. We'll vanish. We'll *disappear*. There'll be no one behind the wheel of this car, you understand?"

A flea market crucifix dangles from the rearview mirror, the prismatic beads glinting in the midmorning sun. I stare at the miniature bronze figure—wondering how a depiction of someone being gruesomely murdered thousands of years ago is supposed to make us feel safe, give us hope, and remind us that every hardship we experience will be worth it in the end.

I glance at my youngest sister in her car seat beside me, grinning her gummy smile and reaching her sticky hands in my direction. Oblivious to the fire-and-brimstone life she's been born into. She doesn't know it yet, but she's in for a wild ride. And maybe she'll never know it, but she deserves better than what's in store for her.

"You listening back there, young lady?" My father peers into the mirror until our eyes meet. I nod. "The Almighty will take us believers to the promised land and leave everyone else behind. And no one knows when. It'll just happen."

It's a story he's told a million times before, like he's been preparing for the end of days his entire life.

My mother frowns as she makes the sign of the cross—her way of emphasizing his point. Rebecca Fielding's role has always been that of his devoted ally; she is a woman of the Almighty first, a wife to Jim second, a dutiful and loyal member of the Church of True Believers third, and somewhere down the line she's our mother.

"*Left behind*, Celia," Dad says with ominous emphasis. Our eyes convene in the rearview once more, and his are a shade of discontent I've seen far too many times before. A chill dances down my spine. "Is that what you want?"

"Of course not," I say.

"What's that?" He taps the top of his ear, a sign for me to speak up. Two decades working in law enforcement have permanently damaged his hearing.

"*Of course not.*" I'm louder this time. I know better than to suggest he turn down the sermon playing from the radio.

"Say it like you mean it, Celia." There's a boom in his voice, a tone I would never question unless *I* wanted to be crucified the second we got home.

"Of. Course. Not," I say a third time, enunciating each and every word at a volume one notch below shouting.

I exchange looks with my younger sister—the one on the other side of Celeste's car seat. Sweet Genevieve is seated perfectly upright, her hands folded neatly in her lap. Her paisley smock dress, slick french braid, and innocent baby blues make her appear younger than her thirteen years.

We both know I'm lying.

We both know I'd give anything to disappear from this life, from this family, from these clothes that itch and constrict. From these oppressive rules that don't make sense. From the skin and voice and eyes and name that feel like they belong to everyone except me.

If I could snap my fingers and be free from all this, I would.

Just like that, I'd be gone.

But I know from personal experience that every action in this family has a dire consequence. If I skip my nightly verse, I'm forced to go without breakfast the next morning. If I accidentally giggle or open my eyes during the pastor's prayers, I'm struck across my lap seven times with a wooden ruler when we get home. If I happen to scan the pews during a sermon and allow my gaze to linger on the green-eyed, wavy-haired Johannsen boy a few seconds too long, I'm sentenced to three days of devotions and water fasting.

My father flicks his turn signal, and we veer into the packed gravel parking lot of the Church of True Believers. We enter the main doors as a family a moment later, the four of us in lockstep as we've done a thousand times, the pink-and-gray car seat hanging from my father's arm.

The sickly sweet scent of pastries and strong coffee fills the air.

Organ music plays low from overhead speakers, a prelude to the three hours of worship ahead of us.

We're greeted with preservice handshakes, blessings, a multitude of *good mornings*, and the friendliest of smiles, all eyes on us. Everyone knows—and loves—the Fieldings. My father is a congregation deacon and ambassador, and Pastor Jacobs often uses us as a shining example of a God-fearing church family.

It seems to me if the God we worship is all-knowing and all-powerful, he would have found a way to let Pastor Jacobs know that we're far from perfect.

We aren't even close.

The overhead song stops—a signal for everyone to take their seats.

Mom takes Celeste to the nursery in the basement.

I follow my father and Genevieve into our usual spot in the second pew on the left, and then I bow my head, mutter the congregational prayer, and half listen as Pastor Jacobs begins today's sermon.

The curls in my hair, the floral pinafore covering my overdeveloped teenage body, the lips that whisper memorized scripture—it all feels like a mask, because how could I ever call myself a child of the Almighty when I'm being raised by the devil himself?

"He does not make us without fault," Pastor Jacobs preaches from his pulpit, sweat already collecting across his brow on this muggy Florida morning. "But where he giveth us darkness, he also giveth us light to show us the way out of that darkness."

"Amen," my father says, lifting his worn leather Bible into the air.

I spend the three hours that follow hatching up a plan to leave once and for all.

This time next week, I'll be gone.

CHAPTER 2

C ELIA

Present day

I watch my husband sleep as if it's the last time I'll ever see him—as if I haven't memorized every bend and arch of his agreeable face and softening middle-aged body a thousand times before under the moon shadows cast from our bedroom window. If I knew it wouldn't wake him, I'd run my fingers through his silky salt-and-pepper hair the way I always do when I'm feeling sentimental.

Sometimes when I can't sleep, I play a little game.

If I died right now—what would be the last words we exchanged? What would his final memory of us be? Would he mourn indefinitely or seek comfort in another's arms before the damp earth anchored my coffin in the ground? Would he remarry? Finally start the family I know he secretly yearns for—albeit later in life? Or would he go on to die of a broken heart? Stress-induced cardiomyopathy is real. I've done the research. My little daydreams are nothing if not accurately portrayed. And I'll admit, it's a sick and twisted game to play for someone who's deathly afraid of . . . *death*.

"Go to sleep." Rob's unexpected interjection sends a start to my chest. He pulls me into his arms, eyes still closed. He doesn't have to look at me to sense me, to know where I am, to reel me into his gravitational orbit.

The bedside clock reads 2:37 AM.

A little more than a half hour ago, we were still mixing and mingling at my fortieth birthday party, surrounded by two decades' worth of treasured friends and associates. We drank the bar dry as a local jazz quartet played tunes made famous by Chet Baker, John Coltrane, and Miles Davis. And we stayed until last call—something we haven't done in ages.

My husband stirs, slightly more awake than before. And then his shoulders press back against our soft mattress as he attempts to find a comfortable position with half my body weight cemented against him. The man would sleep in any contorted situation necessary as long as it meant I was snug.

"You okay?" His breath warms the top of my head.

"Too much excitement tonight, I guess," I whisper, sliding my arm over his chest and watching the way it softly rises and falls. "We had quite the turnout."

With his eyes half-open, he glides his fingers through my hair, sweeping the messy auburn strands off my shoulder until they drape down my back. I reach up and pluck an errant bobby pin I must have missed when I was taking down my french twist earlier. And then I squeeze it tight in my palm, until it's sure to leave an indentation.

"You sure that's it?" He yawns.

"Yeah. We'll talk more at breakfast," I say because he's never been a morning person and anything less than seven hours of sleep turns him into a grizzly bear of a man. Besides, my insomnia has been rearing its merciless head lately for reasons I have yet to pinpoint. It's always a something in a sea of other somethings. My anxieties rotate on a never-ending carousel. For as long as I can remember, an unsettled sensation has resided in the pit of my stomach, though sometimes it takes up occupancy in my chest, and other times it loiters in my head. But it never leaves. It's always there. Like background noise.

I wait for Rob's breath to steady before diving back into my dark reverie—this one involving a lonely widow with soft green eyes who approaches him at a support group for the grieving. And that's exactly the sort of thing Rob would do . . . network with others. His extroverted tendencies would never allow him to be alone for very long, broken heart or no. And I love him too much to wish him a lifetime of loneliness on my account.

The ceiling fan whirs overhead, the pull chain clinking against the glass light fixture in the middle. I make a mental note to adjust it after breakfast.

Rob releases a soft snore—out cold.

What I wouldn't give to simply close my eyes and escape my busy thoughts.

Rising carefully so as not to wake him, I slide out of his arms, out of the warm covers that held us together, and tiptoe downstairs. A doctor once told me the worst thing I could do during bouts of insomnia was lie in bed and not sleep . . . something about training my brain to stay awake in the wrong places. Her best advice was to wear myself out—and the moment I feel exhaustion sinking into my bones, stop everything I'm doing and return to bed.

I wander the main floor like a ghost, floating from room to room in pitch darkness without making a sound—a skill I've honed over the years so as not to worry Rob during particularly restless nights like this.

Eventually I end up in the dining room. But not before going around the main floor and ensuring all the blinds are closed. I'm not sure what it is, but lately I've felt watched. It tends to happen out of nowhere. I'll be in the middle of a task, minding my own business, and a chill will run down my spine or a heaviness will linger in the air, a dark energy of sorts. It's the only way I know how to describe it. The imagination can be a powerful thing, but something about this sensation feels like it's coming from outside me rather than within.

I peek out from behind the dining room curtains for assurance, exhaling a relaxed sigh when I find nothing but an empty street lit by stars, the moon, and a few post lights.

Switching on the overhead chandelier, I dial down the brightness and take a seat in front of the vibrant spread of birthday gifts, cards, floral arrangements, and confetti-filled balloons we hauled home after the party.

I was so busy mixing and mingling and ensuring everyone had equal time with me that I didn't get a chance to open a thing—not that I'm complaining. As a child, we didn't celebrate birthdays the traditional way. We'd spend the day in dedicated service to the church, a way of showing our gratitude for being given the gift of life.

As an adult, I've always found it awkward to open gifts in front of people, as if I'm expected to put on some sort of crowd-pleasing performance. But despite Rob's invitations, which clearly stated "no gifts please," not a single guest showed up empty handed.

I reach for a card in a pale pink envelope, then gently tear the seal and slide out an ornate, foil-covered card. A gift card to one of our favorite local restaurants slips out. I catch it before reading the inscription.

To Celia—

Forty trips around the sun—here's to forty more! Hope you're free for dinner next Friday at seven because we made reservations. Can't wait to catch up!

Your dear friends,

Neal and Deanna Kenworth

PS—Thank you for organizing the meal train last month when Deanna was recovering from her treatments!

I place the card and its contents aside and work on the next one, which contains a generous gift card to a local nail salon.

The third card is from my hairstylist, Deirdre, who has become a close confidante over the years. The first thing she told me when she walked in tonight was that she wouldn't miss my party for the world.

The fourth comes from our next-door neighbors, the Huntingtons, and includes a substantial voucher to a local home-and-garden center. Mrs. Huntington is always complimenting my blue hydrangeas, and I swear I made her year when I finally confessed that the key to their vibrant sky-blue tone was putting pennies in the soil at the base of each plant. Ever since then, she doesn't miss an opportunity to talk home gardening with me.

The fifth card is attached to a flower arrangement—fragrant peonies the color of undriven snow.

Dearest C—

Exquisite blooms for the most exquisite woman I know. Thank you for being a true friend. I don't know what I'd have done without you these last few years. So grateful to have you in my life. Can't wait for our girls' trip next month and hope forty is your most incredible year yet! Let's make it one for the books . . .

Natalie xo

I take a break from cards and work on opening a few gifts, moving first for the one covered in an extravagant amount of shiny, curled ribbons and wrapped in paper so ostentatious it surely cost a pretty penny. I don't need to look at the label to know it's from Monique Denman—a local interior designer so well known for her gift-wrapping talents that people book her years in advance to do their Christmas gifts. I first met her fifteen years back, when we were in over our heads on a kitchen renovation. She came highly recommended by someone I knew, and by the end of the project, we'd become fast friends.

A moment later, I'm unboxing a breathtaking cut-crystal vase—one I've seen in the window display of a local jewelry store. I've had my eye on it for months, never quite ready to pull the trigger because I couldn't justify the hefty price tag.

A small note rests at the bottom of the piece, curled into a scroll and secured by a tiny ribbon.

C—

Happy 40th birthday . . . and happy 15th friend-i-versary. Is that a thing? It is now.

Love, love, love—

M

Monique is too kind.

I admire the beautiful work of art, letting its facets dance in the subdued light before carefully placing it aside and working on the next gift in the pile.

Fifteen minutes later, I've unboxed a sapphire tennis bracelet from Margaux Mansfield and a case of gourmet snacks from Adam and Clint Bradbury. From Angelica Steiner, a plush robe from my favorite spa. A bottle of vintage Veuve Clicquot and European chocolates from Serena Briese.

I'm not sure what I did to deserve this outpouring of adoration. Truly. All my life, people have gravitated toward me, spilled their deepest secrets, and kept me near and dear to their hearts.

Rob says everyone appreciates having me in their life because I ask questions and always let them be the center of any conversation. He says people love to talk about themselves, and as an introvert, I'm a natural-born listener. I suppose he's right, but it's never been something I've done to intentionally win people over.

I simply don't enjoy talking about myself.

There was only ever one person who got to know me, and whom I let my guard down around, because she was the only person I'd ever met who looked at me and didn't see Rob Guest's childless, stay-at-home, younger wife. Nor did she see the president of the Willowmere Homeowners' Association, a standing member of the local Kiwanis club, or the founder of the Schofield, Connecticut, Social Club. To her, I wasn't that quiet homemaker whom everyone knew for the delectable strawberry-rhubarb crumble she brought to Bunco the first Monday of each month.

Isabel simply saw . . . *me*.

I return to the stack of birthday cards, flipping through the remaining pile in search of familiar handwriting.

Rob mentioned he'd invited Isabel and her husband, though he never received an RSVP. I'd be lying if I said I hadn't foolishly hoped she'd show up anyway, greet me with a warm embrace, and tell me everything that happened two months ago was water under the bridge.

I think about her every day.

I miss her presence in my life more than she'll ever know.

As my life ticks on without her, I catch myself having imaginary conversations with her, wishing we could go back to the way it was for just one more day.

I'd never had a friend quite like Isabel before—something like a best friend–sister hybrid, and I doubt I ever will again.

When Rob and I moved Genevieve and her family here a couple of years ago, I'd hoped the two of us would be able to reconnect, to grow close again. But at times, I wonder if it only made the emotional distance between us more profound than ever.

My stomach knots when I think about the empty chair at one of the high-top tables at the party. Gen initially said she'd come, but she wanted to invite our youngest sister as well. Celeste was four when I left Cross Beach, and we haven't spoken since. We're strangers and sisters—an unfortunate combination. While I doubt Celeste remembers me, she serves as a reminder of the life I left behind all those years back.

I told Gen I wasn't feeling up to a family reunion just yet, which prompted an argument I wasn't prepared for. The words we exchanged were unkind on both sides, colored by a complicated family history that would take a lifetime of expensive therapy to unravel.

While the three of us grew up in the same house, with the same parents, each of our experiences couldn't be more different.

Maybe someday we can all sit down and hash things out—but a birthday celebration wasn't the time or place.

Genevieve, however, disagreed profusely. Now we're going on almost a month of not speaking—which I suppose is a drop in the ocean compared to the decades we went without talking before that.

Sorting through the remaining stack, I rip the seal on a small navy-blue envelope. Only there isn't a card inside. Instead, it's a creased letter. Unfolding it, I'm met with a slip of lined stationery with a floral William Morris design around the perimeter. Below it, a single sentence scribed in thick black marker, all caps.

YOU DON'T DESERVE ANY OF THIS.

Beneath that is **JUNE 14th**—yesterday's date.

My birth date.

It's underlined twice and circled.

My breath shallows as I read over the cruel message from a partygoer who conveniently neglected to sign their name. Frantic, I sort through the pile of cards and gifts, mentally matching them up with every person in attendance tonight.

Everyone is accounted for.

CHAPTER 3

GENEVIEVE

Present day

I page through a worn library book—some sensational World War II romance that was all the rage a few years back—in an attempt to be anywhere but here.

While my sister and her husband celebrate her fortieth birthday with drinks, live music, and friends in some upscale bar in the trendy part of town, I'm sitting in holey pajamas, paging through this doorstop of a novel while I wait for my daughter to text me to pick her up from a local baseball game.

"Going to top off my wine." I rise from my spot on our sagging sofa, turning to my husband in his recliner. "Need me to grab you anything?"

It takes a moment for me to realize he's passed out. I take the half-empty beer bottle from his hand and place it on a coaster. Lord knows if it falls and douses the carpet, I'll be the one cleaning it up.

I refill my wineglass and make a laughable excuse for a charcuterie board with a stack of RITZ crackers, sliced bologna sausage, a few squares of American cheese, and a handful of green grapes. And then I return to the living room, to my snoring husband, to my quiet, lamplit Friday night.

Before getting back into my book, I grab my phone off the coffee table and fire off a text to my younger sister, Celeste. Just a little something to tell her I'm thinking of her—and a roundabout way of letting her know I skipped out on Celia's party.

Last month, when I told Celeste about the get-together, she suggested that she buy a plane ticket to Connecticut and surprise Celia. While I agreed that Celeste should attend—it's her sister, for crying out loud—I didn't agree with springing it on Celia like that.

When I spoke with Celia the following day and mentioned inviting Celeste, I wasn't expecting to be met with a resounding "no." Something about how she isn't ready yet and she hardly knows Celeste and it would be weird to see her for the first time in decades in that sort of a setting. I told her she was overthinking it. She told me I was being presumptuous. The rest of the conversation is a blur I'd rather not remember. All I know now is it's been a month since we last spoke, and it's anyone's guess when we'll speak again.

Since moving here two years ago to reconnect with Celia, I've yet to shake the guilt I've felt at leaving Celeste behind. Celeste has never said anything—that's not her style—but I'm sure a part of her felt left out. If I had something to show for these efforts, maybe I'd feel slightly better about it, but Celia's been as distant here as she was back home. At times, it's as if she's abandoning me all over again.

I'm hopeful that with time, the three of us can be a family again—without the undercurrent of an overzealous religion.

Few things in this life are as sacred as sisterhood.

CHAPTER 4

GENEVIEVE

Twenty-five years ago

"Have you seen Celia?" Mom stands in the living room doorway as I bounce my baby sister on my lap. "Can't find that girl anywhere."

"Did you look out back behind the shed?" I ask. "She said something about picking the peas earlier."

The yeasty smell of baking dinner rolls fills the air, and Mom wipes her hands on her apron.

"She's not outside," she says. "I've looked in the garage, in the shed . . ."

Shaking her head, she wanders off, talking to herself out loud.

Celeste grabs a fistful of my hair, shoving it in her mouth.

"No, no." I gently take the wet strands from her grasp and tuck them behind my ear. The dampness is disgusting, but what can I do? I grab a teething toy from the coffee table, which seems to do the trick as she squeals and claps. "Should we try to find our sister before she lands herself in hot water again?"

I hoist the baby on my hip as we make our way around the house, checking closets and cupboards, nooks and crannies. I wind up in the kitchen when I'm finished, where our mother is transferring the baked rolls into a basket with a red gingham tea towel.

"Any luck?" she asks.

I place Celeste in her high chair before filling a sippy cup with milk from a near-empty jug.

"Nope," I say. "Maybe she went to the store for milk and took the long way home?"

It wouldn't be the first time.

Celia will do anything for an extra couple of minutes out from underneath this roof. Not that I blame her. Mom and Dad's rules are oppressive sometimes, but other times I think things aren't as bad as Celia makes them out to be. As long as we keep quiet and do what we're told, it's a pretty peaceful existence.

Mom turns around, shooting me a look with one eyebrow arched high. "Now, Genevieve. You know better than to go making excuses for that girl. Go ahead and set the table. If your sister's not home in five minutes, we're eating without her and she can go to bed hungry."

This wouldn't be the first time.

It won't be the last either.

Celia has a knack for getting herself into trouble.

I grab plates and silverware from the cupboard and set the table, making sure to give Celia the plate with the blue flowers. Her favorite. Sometimes I try and do a few nice things for my sister to counteract all the bad things my parents do to her.

The washing machine chimes from the laundry room down the hall.

"I'll get it," I say before my mother tells me to. I've gotten good at anticipating the things she's going to say before she says them lately— like dodging verbal land mines.

I'm transferring the load into the dryer when I hear the back door swing open and slam shut, and I return to the kitchen just in time to hear Mom giving Celia an oral lashing.

"Where's Dad?" I interrupt in an attempt to de-escalate the situation. "Isn't he usually home by now?"

Mom glances at the clock on the oven. She won't hesitate to send Celia to bed with an empty stomach for being late to dinner, but never in a million years would we start a meal without my father there to bless the food first. Grabbing the cordless phone off its base, Mom dials Dad's number, one hand perched on her hip as she peers out the window above the sink.

"Thank you," Celia mouths to me.

We've always had an unspoken understanding.

I nod, a silent way of reminding her that we're in this together.

Celeste bangs her sippy cup against her tray, and I gently coerce it out of her chubby hands. Mom hates racket of any kind. She says it gives her headaches.

"He's on his way home," Mom says, ending her call. "Celia, go wash your hands. Lord only knows where you've been."

Celia heads to the bathroom to wash up, and I take the spot next to the high chair. Feeding the baby has always been my duty, while Celia was supposed to be the one giving her baths, but inevitably I'm the one who does most of the tending. Mom is always cooking or cleaning, Dad is always at work, and Celia's always . . . gone.

CHAPTER 5

Celia

Twenty-five years ago

"Your parents are okay with this?" I ask Rachel Carmichael as I peruse her nail polish collection. My eyes are wide, and my heart's beating so hard in my chest I'm sure her mom can hear it in the next room over.

To say my parents are big on modesty would be an understatement, but I was invited to Rachel Carmichael's house after church today with both our parents' blessings, and she suggested we paint our nails the instant we got settled.

Making friends has never been easy for me. My parents have a million rules, and no one wants to hang out with the girl who can't do anything. Given that the Carmichaels are the newest family to join our church, I could tell my parents were trying to be gracious by allowing me to spend the afternoon with Rachel. It was all in an effort to make them feel welcome, I'm sure. The bigger our congregation, the more mouths there are to spread our teachings.

Rachel's bedroom is like something out of a movie scene. Pink polka-dot bedspread, a stack of teen magazines on her nightstand, and a purple-and-aqua Caboodle filled with every color of nail polish under the sun. It smells like raspberry body spray and Coppertone sunscreen. And the hamper in the corner is overflowing with the kind of clothes you buy at an actual mall—not the secondhand thrift finds or humble church garb I'm accustomed to.

Rachel chuckles, plucking a shade of Dare Me pink from one of the top compartments and angling it my way.

"They don't care," she says with a confident shrug. "As long as I take it off before church, I can wear it whenever I want."

I accept the shiny glass bottle with the white cap, hands shaking, feeling as though I'm handling a cigarette—or worse. Not that I would know what that feels like, but my father has shared many a terrifying tale of the types of drug addicts he comes into contact with on a daily basis on patrol.

"I probably shouldn't," I say.

"Have you ever had your nails painted?" she asks, a single white-blonde brow raised. Before I can answer, she selects a glittery orange-red bottle, unscrews the cap, and paints her thumbnail. "See? It's really not a big deal. It's just color."

After that, she pulls out a small plastic jar, twists the lid, and dips her thumb inside. When she pulls it out, the polish is gone—as if it had never been there in the first place.

"Come on." A mischievous smile covers her face. "Let's do your nails. We'll take it off before your parents come to pick you up."

Rachel's blonde ringlets bounce with every step as she sets up a little station on the top of her dresser. Nail clippers. A file. An assortment of other tools. She lays them out the way I imagine a surgeon's assistant would lay out scalpels and drills. It all looks like contraband.

And feels like otherworldly magic.

Like sparkles dance through every part of me before settling in my fingers and toes.

My stomach swirls with anticipation, but my excitement overrides any nausea that threatens to rise up my throat.

Before she begins, she puts some music on—something I've never heard before. Something that sounds an awful lot like the sort of thing that would get me a severe lashing in the back shed . . . one that would make sitting an impossible task for the foreseeable future.

"You're tense," she says with a giggle, as though she's amused. "Relax, Celia."

"Sorry. I'm just not used to this," I say.

"Don't be sorry," she says before singing the chorus of whatever this song is under her breath. "Your church is super strict. Our church now, I guess. My parents are still testing it out. Mom says she's still on the fence, but don't tell Pastor Jacobs."

"Testing it out?" I ask, as the concept is foreign to me. To my parents, uncertainty and questioning are the work of the devil. You're either with us or against us. And if you're against us, you're damned to hell.

"Yeah, we're just seeing if we like it." Rachel paints the last nail on my left hand before moving to my right. The brash yet glossy pink is like mesmerizing eye candy. My heart trots in my chest as I watch her paint on additional strokes of saturated pink liquid.

"Where will you go if you don't like it?" I ask. Almost everyone in Cross Beach attends the Church of True Believers. Anyone who doesn't is treated like an outsider, a modern-day leper. There are small businesses in this town who will refuse to assist someone they don't recognize from the Sunday services. I've witnessed it more times than I can count.

Rachel shrugs as the song changes. A female with a breathy, baby-soft voice begins crooning from the speakers, singing something about hitting her one more time. I can't quite grasp the meaning of the lyrics, but the song makes me feel alive in a weird way—like enjoying a Bomb Pop on a hot summer's day, not a care in the world.

My muscles clench at the thought of my parents knowing I'm listening to this sort of thing. And then I relax, realizing they'd never know unless I told them. And I would never breathe a word of this.

When Rachel is finished, she blows on my left hand while I blow on my right.

Five minutes later, the polish is set, the color a bold statement where my pale, flesh-toned nail beds once were, but I can't get enough. My father is supposed to pick me up in two hours, and I intend to wear this until the moment his tires crunch against the gravel of the Carmichael driveway.

It gives me a sense of . . . poise. Makes me feel older, in a way. And dare I say . . . emboldened?

"Have you read the newest *Seventeen* yet?" Rachel tosses me a colorful magazine with a beautiful girl on the cover, one with a full face of makeup, one who appears happy, free, and unencumbered by a myriad of never-ending rules. "Oh. Are you not allowed to read these?" She plops onto the foot of her bed. "I won't tell if you won't?"

I trace my glinting fingertips over the glossy cover, and it takes all the strength I have not to tear through it and devour each page in record speed. But all I can hear are my father's words in the back of my mind, lecturing me about forbidden fruit and retelling the story of Eve and the serpent in the Garden of Eden.

I chuckle under my breath.

If Rachel's room is the Garden of Eden and this magazine is forbidden fruit, that would make Rachel the serpent. She's far from a serpent. She's jovial and carefree, and all she wants is for me to have a good time.

I've never been around someone like her before.

In a flicker of a second, I envision a best friendship with her, the two of us sharing secrets, curling each other's hair, and talking about the kinds of things only girlfriends talk about.

I bite my bottom lip, contemplating my next move. I'm not sure what could be in these pages that could be so wicked and vile that my parents forbade my sister and me from so much as glancing toward the magazine racks at the grocery store. *Sin rags,* they call them. *Fire kindling.*

"What's . . . in this?" I let my curiosity get the best of me. I can't help myself.

Rachel blows an ice-blonde tendril from her forehead, leaning back and steadying herself on her palms. "Um, I don't know. Like . . . fashion. Advice. Ads for tampons and lip gloss. Makeup tips. Oh! They have a whole page of embarrassing moments. I always read that section first."

None of those things sound evil.

"If you don't want to read it, no biggie," she says, studying me. I'm sure my reluctance is wafting off me thanks to the damp half moons of perspiration forming under my arms by the second.

Before I can respond, there's a knock at her door.

"Celia? Your father is here," Mrs. Carmichael calls from the other side.

My gaze snaps to the daisy-shaped alarm clock on her nightstand. He's early.

Rebecca and I lock eyes, hers holding confusion and mine holding sheer terror.

"Do you have that remover stuff?" I ask in a whisper, scanning the scattered mess on her dresser top.

"Celia?" Her mom opens the door, and I stand frozen, my jaw hanging open and my hands clenched behind my back as shame and fear take center stage.

I exhale when I realize my father isn't standing behind her.

Without missing a beat, Rachel rises from her bed and dials down her music. "Sorry, Mom. We didn't hear you. I thought her dad was coming later?"

Mrs. Carmichael shrugs, as if to say her guess is as good as ours. "Well, he's here now, and he said they needed to get going."

The sound of her dad and mine making small talk floats from down the hall. He's inside. He's waiting for me. There isn't time to remove the polish.

Sweat collects across my brow, but I gather a long, hard breath, shove my sinful hands in the pockets of my pinafore, and head to the front entry. Each step echoes against their bare walls. Mrs. Carmichael made a point of telling me they're still getting unpacked and have yet to so much as think about decorating the place. She seemed to care what I thought about the house, which struck me as funny at the time—an adult woman worried that a fifteen-year-old girl might judge her house as less than perfect. But there's nothing funny about anything now. The humor is sucked out of me like marrow from a bone.

"Hi, Father," I say, holding my eyes on his and praying he doesn't look down and wonder why my hands are hidden.

"Celia, what do you say to the Carmichaels?" he asks.

I turn to Rachel's parents. "Thank you for having me over. I had a lovely time."

"Can Celia hang out again sometime?" Rachel asks my father. I'm the only one who catches his microwince at the words "hang out." Hanging out is too informal for his liking. He'd much prefer words like "congregate" and "visit."

But his eyes soften, and for a moment, he looks like the version of my father that everyone knows and loves: the gentle, six-foot-four police officer with a disarming blue gaze and the sweetest daughters in all of Cross Beach.

"Of course," he tells her.

I can't tell if he's lying. I can only hope he isn't.

"Celia." He places a hand on my shoulder and gives it a squeeze. "We best get going now."

I ride in the back seat on the way home, where I always sit, grateful to keep my hands in my pockets a little longer. I don't ask why he picked me up early—I can only assume it had something to do with him not knowing the Carmichaels and not having complete control over every second of my existence for too long.

For the following seven minutes, I scrape my fingernails against the polish, praying I'm scratching the thick pink color off layer by layer. But when we get home, most of it's still there. I haven't made but a handful of chips and dents.

Heading straight for the bathroom, I wash my hands under the hottest water, scrubbing them with a bristled brush until the skin around my nails turns almost as pink as the polish itself.

Nothing helps.

If anything, I'm making it ten times as obvious as before.

"Celia? Everything okay in there?" My mother's voice presses through the bathroom door.

"Of course," I call back, shutting the water off and drying my hands. The towel is rough against my tender cuticles.

"When you're finished, I've got a sink full of dishes that need to be washed," she says.

"Yes, Mother. I'll be right out." I wait for the creak of the floor to tell me she's moved on, and then I emerge a minute later, quietly shuffle to the kitchen, and bury my hands in the soapy dishwater waiting for me.

"Did you have a nice time with the Carmichael girl?" My mother's voice startles me from behind. I was so consumed by the chore at hand, I hadn't heard her coming.

"Yes," I say. "She's very nice."

"And what did the two of you do?" She retrieves a can of tomatoes from the pantry, followed by a can of green beans and corn, and then she places them next to the slow cooker.

"We just hung out—*visited*—in her room," I say.

"Did you talk about anything?" She's fishing for information.

"I wasn't there very long . . . We didn't have time to talk about much of anything, really." I scrub a dish under the protective cover of bubbles. "She mostly just talked about being new around here and getting settled."

"Do they like the church?" Her tone is laced with hope.

Rachel's words about testing it out play in the front of my mind, but I know better than to disappoint my mother when it comes to the thing she loves most in this world.

I clear my throat. "I believe so."

Mom grabs a can opener from a drawer, gently sliding it shut. "Well, that's lovely to hear. They seem like a great family, and I know Pastor Jacobs thinks very highly of them already."

My heart tromps against my chest wall as I lift the ceramic dinner plate I've been scrubbing the last two minutes out of the water. I give it a quick rinse before placing it on the drying rack.

"Celia Joy, what on earth is on your fingernails?" My mother swipes at my hands before I get a chance to dunk them back into the gray-brown dishwater. She grips them so hard I yelp. *"Nail polish?"*

The smack of her palm against my left cheek happens so fast I don't have a chance to react, but thanks to the cocktail of fear and adrenaline coursing through my veins, I don't even feel it.

"Jim. Jim, come in here," she calls, her tone eerily calm yet her words urgent at the same time.

The sound of my father's work boots tromping down the hallway comes to a hard stop when he reaches the entrance of the kitchen.

"What's going on?" he asks, dressed in full blues, which means he's going into work tonight—likely picking up an extra shift, which he does from time to time so he can donate his overtime to the church.

If only he'd left earlier.

"We have a liar and a sinner on our hands, that's what's going on." My mother steps back, arms crossed, a move I've seen before. It's the same one she makes when she's about to let my father take the reins. "Go on, Celia. Show him what you did at that Carmichael girl's house."

My father's brows meet in the middle.

I lift my hands, my skin raw and my fingertips trembling—my guilt practically spelled out for them in capital letters with a neon sign.

I don't have to guess what will happen next.

I already know.

A lecture, a beating, a night in the hell shed—the makeshift hades on earth my parents have set up over the years to keep Genevieve and me on the right path. Twenty-four hours in a hot, dark, dank, windowless four-by-six space with nothing but a single bottle of water and a five-gallon bucket should I need to relieve myself . . . though I try not to unless I can't help it.

The baby cries from her crib down the hall, and my mother vanishes, leaving me alone with the devil himself.

By the time my father secures the padlock on the shed an hour later, my backside is hotter than fire, and I can feel the throb of bruises forming on the backs of my arms in real time.

He mutters a prayer—begging God to have mercy on my soul, pleading for him to forgive us both. He promises he'll do better, that he'll raise me right . . . whatever it takes. And no prayer is complete without him thanking the good lord for giving him Celeste—his God-given second chance at getting it right.

I spend the day that follows begging God to put me out of my misery—or to at least let me leave.

My parents send Genevieve to unlock the shed Monday afternoon. She won't make eye contact with me, and she doesn't say a word during the thirty-yard trek back to the house. She knows better.

I shower off twenty-four hours' worth of sweat, tears, and grime, and when I'm finished, I examine the bruises that cover my body while my parents' words play in my mind, telling me I'm worthless, unlikable, and walking the narrow path to the fiery gates of hell where I belong.

Six more days and I'll be gone.

CHAPTER 6

CELIA

Present day

I pace the main floor for a solid hour, all but wearing a pattern in the floor by the time I come to a stop at the kitchen island. I've replayed bits and pieces of my party to the best of my recollection, analyzing various conversations through a different lens. My memory is hazy thanks to all the free-flowing wine, my feet ache from standing in my highest heels tonight, and my face still hurts from smiling, but I won't rest—physically, mentally, or otherwise—until I've dissected this every which way possible . . . because the problem is, whoever wrote that note? They weren't wrong.

I don't disagree with them. Not for a second.

I think back to Deanna Kenworth's smile earlier, how it seemed painted on, appearing only when our eyes locked and then fading the instant she looked away. Then again, she's been battling a lymphoma for the past several months. She's exhausted and doing her best to keep up with her social schedule. I imagine it's taken a toll on her and it was a big feat just to get dressed and put on a happy face among friends.

Holly and Peter stayed long enough to enjoy a few hors d'oeuvres and one martini each before jetting off, blaming their babysitter for their short appearance. Ordinarily I wouldn't take that personally, but now . . .

Deirdre seemed distracted, checking her phone every five minutes as if she were waiting for a call or text. I assumed she and her on-again, off-again beau were on the outs and perhaps they were fighting, so I thought nothing of it. In retrospect, maybe she was hoping for an excuse to leave?

And then there was Margaux, who wasn't her typical bubbly self. Not once did she chat my ear off like usual. I was planning on asking her if everything was okay, but then I got sidetracked by Adam Bradbury, who wanted to tell me a funny story about the quiche recipe I gave him two Christmases ago.

I lean over the gleaming quartzite countertop, its marbled veins reflecting off the faint undercabinet lighting of our dark kitchen. With a hand haphazardly over my mouth, I exhale through my nose as I mentally replay my conversation with Natalie. She's become one of my closest friends these past few years, all of it starting when she left her husband of ten years. We'd met at the Kiwanis club shortly before that, and she was new in town. She wasn't normally into community organizations like that, but she didn't know a soul in Schofield and thought she might find a few friendly faces there. Natalie grinned ear to ear when she walked in tonight, that giant bouquet of white peonies in hand, and she air-kissed my cheeks before staring me deep in the eyes and wishing me the happiest birthday. She told me she loved me and that she was so grateful our paths crossed exactly when they did. I wasted no time ordering her favorite drink for her—a paloma, extra salt—before introducing her to my hairstylist, who was also there alone.

A handful of moments, I caught Natalie staring my way, a neutral expression on her face. As much as she has embraced her new lease on life these last few years, she's also confessed to feeling a gnawing, aching loneliness at times. At one point, I glanced her way and found her sipping her grapefruit cocktail surrounded by a sea of happy couples—the Harringtons, the Bradburys, the Kenworths . . .

Still, she's never so much as hinted at feeling resentment toward me or my life.

It couldn't have been Natalie.

Monique, Serena, and Angelica spent most of the evening chatting up a storm—and while I was grateful that they were enjoying themselves, a part of me felt a pang of disappointment when Monique asked me to introduce her to my sister. I'm a terrible liar, but I managed to come up with an excuse for her on the fly—blaming it on a stubborn cold so I didn't have to go into detail about the fight we had last week.

Genevieve and I haven't always seen eye to eye. Our childhood was different. I couldn't get away from Cross Beach—or my parents—fast enough, but in retrospect, I left my sisters behind to fend for themselves.

It's something I've spent my adult lifetime regretting, though I haven't always articulated that the best to her. The conversations we've had about it over the years usually ended in tears and one of us hanging up on the other. And I've yet to reach out to Celeste, though I think of her often. It's been so long I don't know what I'd say if I called her now—or if she'd even want to hear from me.

Sisterhood is a messy, beautiful, complex kaleidoscope of emotions.

They say no one will ever know you, love you, or drive you to madness quite like a sister will. I'm hopeful that one of these days we'll get back what we once had—minus the terrifying levels of dysfunction we grew up with.

I take a seat at the kitchen island, slumping over and exhaling a long, hard breath.

Assumptions are a slippery slope, and I've never been one to take things personally. From a young age, it was all but beaten into me that the world doesn't revolve around me—not even for a second. Besides, at forty years old, I should be long past the phase of caring what others think of me.

But knowing that someone came to my party tonight, wished me happy birthday, then imparted a cruel little one-liner is akin to an emotional sucker punch. It's a below-the-belt hit that could only stem from deep, harbored resentment.

A stack of mail to my left catches my attention, slowly siphoning me out of my thoughts for a brief moment. At the top of that stack rests Rob's official job offer—an administrator position at a hospital in Kansas City, Missouri. It's an impressive proposal, one that would be difficult for anyone to turn down. But we're in a fortunate enough position that we aren't hurting for money. This move would have nothing to do with anything other than the fact that Rob, at fifty-three, is craving a change of scenery.

Never mind the life we've built here.

He didn't tell me he applied for the position at all—or that he'd been looking. He simply came home one day and sprang his job offer on me over a dinner of beef Wellington and roasted vegetables, like it was any other Thursday.

I hid my initial reaction with a generous sip of wine, and then I took a deep breath, offered a loving smile, and pretended to be happy for him—for *us*.

I don't want to leave Schofield.

I've lived here for the past twenty years . . . I intended on dying here, too.

But in true Celia Guest fashion, I told him yes.

I told him to accept the position—and I did it with a smile on my face because when you love someone, their happiness is supposed to be yours.

Given the fact that I'm not a contributing member of this household—at least financially speaking—and I hadn't seen his eyes so lit in years, it seemed wrong to dig my heels into the ground without giving it deeper thought.

Rob, who was clearly nervous about my reaction, wasted no time pushing his chair out, rushing to my end of the table, pulling me into his arms, and spinning me in celebration.

"And this is why I love you so," he said before he stole a deep, hard kiss.

He's nothing if not an old-fashioned romantic, my husband.

We've been inseparable from the day we met—age difference be damned.

But in that moment, all I could do was wonder if I knew him as well as I thought I did.

He claimed he didn't tell me about his job interview because he didn't expect to get the position and didn't want to worry me. I was less concerned with that and more concerned with the fact that Rob was feeling so restless about the cozy life we'd built together that he wanted to move 1,300 miles away and start fresh.

The idea of leaving all this behind—our friends, our home, our community—made me sick with worry for weeks afterward, and a handful of times I considered asking him to turn the position down. He hasn't officially accepted it yet, as they're still ironing out the details of the offer as well as negotiating his benefits package. Not to mention, we spent all that time and effort relocating my sister, her husband, and their daughter to Schofield two years ago—it wouldn't be right to leave them behind.

But now . . . knowing that perhaps people don't think of me the way I thought they did, the idea of someone speaking ill about me behind my back when all I've done is happily bend over backward for every person in my circle . . . that changes things. Perhaps it's dramatic to want to pick up and leave all because of a ridiculous little note—but it certainly shakes the foundation on which I've painstakingly built my reputation, my *life*.

I only wish I knew if their sentiments were coming from a resentful place . . . or a place of knowing the past from which I've been running my entire life.

Everyone has secrets.

Some stay buried.

Some are unearthed when you least expect.

If someone knew where I came from—what I've done—it would be fair to say I don't deserve any of this.

With each jagged breath, the walls close in around me until breathing becomes an unbearable task.

I need air.

I need space.

I need to leave—just for a little while.

I reach for a nearby pen and scrawl a note to my husband on the back of the envelope that contains his job offer.

Rob—

Gone out. Be back soon . . .

Celia

I toss my phone in my purse, slip into a pair of tennis shoes by the back door, tie a zip-up hoodie around my waist, grab a baseball cap to cover my messy hair, and quietly tiptoe to the driveway. A minute later, I'm backing out, the electric engine of my SUV quiet as a church mouse.

I roll the windows down, gulping in the tepid night air that rustles my hair and kisses my face, but every time I blink—every time I close my eyes for even a fraction of a second—I see that note.

I'm five streets away before my breath finally steadies and that dreadful suffocating sensation begins to dissipate. With nothing but road noise, whistling wind, and a clear, starry sky to comfort me, I remind myself I'm alive and that's all that matters in this very moment.

But for now, I keep driving.

CHAPTER 7

GENEVIEVE

Twenty-five years ago

"I've got a mountain of homework tonight. You mind doing her bath?" Celia hands me a wiggly Celeste after dinner before strutting down the hall and closing herself in her room.

Same excuse as always, different night.

I debate telling her no this time, just to see what she'd say. Sometimes I wonder if she's jealous of Celeste and all the attention she gets at church—or if she's just trying to get out of doing chores.

With the baby on my hip, I head to her room and rap lightly on her door.

A moment later it springs open.

"Yeah?" Celia asks.

"It's just . . . you haven't given her a bath in weeks. I've been doing them all lately," I say as the intensity of her gaze bores into me. "There's a show on tonight that I wanted to watch, and it starts in ten minutes."

Celia's eyes roam to Celeste, and she exhales. "Fine." She reaches for the baby, who begins to cling to me when she realizes what's going on. "She doesn't want me to take her. She wants you."

I can't help it that I'm Celeste's favorite.

"Please?" I ask my older sister.

She doesn't answer, but she reaches for Celeste once more, prying her off me.

"Sometimes I think she hates me," Celia says, carrying her to the hall bath.

I follow behind, biting my tongue, because all I want to do is remind her that Celeste wouldn't "hate" her if she actually made time for her for once.

From the moment Celeste arrived, Celia has been cold and distant to her. Disengaged and uninterested. When my father pointed it out once, Celia claimed that she didn't like babies. Without hesitation, he backhanded her across the mouth before calmly reminding her that babies are a *blessing from God*.

The numbers of diapers Celia has changed in the past year, I could probably count on one hand. The number of bottles she's fed Celeste, I could maybe count on my fingers and toes.

It's not fair that Celia gets away with doing nothing while I get stuck doing everything, but I know better than to point out the discrepancy to my parents. They'll punish her and she'll dislike me even more than she already does.

I miss the days when we were friends and not just sisters. It wasn't that long ago that we would walk home from the bus stop together, hand in hand, singing silly rhymes and making up little games to pass the time. It was a mere three-block trek, but I loved every minute of it. It was always the highlight of my day.

But something has changed in Celia.

These days she walks a handful of steps ahead of me on the way home. She shuts herself in her room or disappears altogether. We used to take turns camping out in each other's rooms every Friday night, sharing stories and playing card games. I can't remember the last time we did that—it must have been before Celeste came.

"I'll put her to bed," I tell Celia as I watch her run the bathwater.

"Okay," is all she says.

I've heard my father say on several occasions that Celia only cares about herself, that she's walking down the road to eternal damnation. If that's the case, I certainly don't want to join her in hell.

Some older sisters teach you what to do. Mine teaches me what *not* to do.

Tonight, when I'm tucking Celeste in and saying our nightly prayers, I'll say one for Celia, too.

CHAPTER 8

CELIA

Twenty-five years ago

I pull an armful of clothes from my backpack and hand them to Rachel outside her locker. Earlier this week, she took me aside at lunch to talk about what happened on Sunday. She asked if I was okay and if my dad was always that "intense." I'm not sure what came over me in that moment, but my tears spilled like a river and so did fifteen years' worth of pent-up *everything*.

I didn't tell her about what happened last summer—that's something I'm taking to the grave.

By the time the lunch bell rang, I'd told her I wanted to run away. She laughed at first, as if I were joking. But I assured her I wasn't.

The following day we ate lunch in the hallway by the library—seeking a little more privacy so I could go into greater detail about my plan. That's when Rachel offered to help.

"I cashed in some savings bonds," she says as she places my clothes into her bag. Packing little by little, day by day, is the only way I'm going to sneak my things out of the house without my parents knowing. "It isn't much, but I want you to have it. You need it more than me."

She jams her hands into her jean shorts pocket and pulls out two hundred-dollar bills and a few twenties.

"You didn't have to do that, Rachel." I don't reach for the money. It doesn't seem right. She's already helping me more than I deserve. But maybe that's what friends do. If our places were switched around, I'd do the same thing for her. She's the closest thing I've ever had to a real friend, and of course we meet during the last week of the school year, the very week I planned to ditch this place.

I hardly know her but I'm going to miss her the most.

"Please," she says, shoving the folded bills at me and practically forcing them into my hand. "I won't take no for an answer."

Come Friday, Rachel will have compiled all my clothes into one of her duffel bags so I can grab them and run. But it won't be that simple. Instead of taking the bus with Genevieve, I'll exit at the east doors of the school and meet Rachel by the giant maple tree on the corner, and then we'll walk home the back way. Once there, she'll sneak me in through the breezeway and I'll hide out in her closet the rest of the evening. Once her parents are in bed, I'll leave under the cover of darkness. There's a bus stop two miles from her house. I've already purchased a ticket to Atlanta—the closest metropolitan hub I could afford with my limited funds. From there, I'll hop on another bus and work my way far from these sandy Floridian shores. If I never see a palm tree again, it'll be too soon.

"Thank you," I say, sliding the money deep into my pocket to ensure it won't fall out.

Tomorrow's the day.

My heart pulsates in my ears with each step toward the maple tree Friday afternoon, drowning out the sounds of kids laughing in the background, car doors slamming shut, and school buses idling.

Rachel is already there, waiting, her eyes darting from side to side as if she's taking note of who might notice us together. She motions for me to hurry up, so I pick up my pace, trotting faster until I'm almost sprinting.

"You ready to do this?" she asks.

I nod, too breathless to say anything.

With our heads tucked, we make our way to the corner. I'm not sure what the "back way" to her house entails, so I follow her lead. She's not as talkative as she usually is, which makes me think she's just as nervous as I am. If her parents catch us, she'll be grounded. Not only that, but she'll be grounded from *me*.

We're three blocks away when we approach a four-way stop.

"Shit," Rachel says. It's the first time I've heard her curse. "Don't look up."

My stomach drops, and for the strangest reason, I look up anyway.

Bus #12 crawls to a stop at the sign closest to us.

My bus . . .

The bus currently taking my sister home . . .

My sister who is probably wondering why I'm not on it . . .

"Shit." I utter that word for the first time in my life. It's wavy on my lips.

Genevieve slams her palms against the glass when she spots me, mouthing words too far away for me to hear.

"Keep walking, keep walking," Rachel says under her breath, her hand on my back.

"What if she tells?"

Rachel doesn't answer at first, as if she needs a moment to process all the ways this could go.

"Maybe she won't?" She shrugs. "Maybe she'll just assume you came home with me because it's the last day of school?"

I worry the inside of my lip, where I've been working the flesh to a blister all week.

"I'll hide you in the guest room," she says. "Under the bed. No one ever goes in there. It's full of boxes my parents still haven't unpacked from the move. If Genevieve says she saw us together, I'll play dumb."

"Genevieve doesn't lie," I say. "My parents will see through that. They'll know."

"Okay, so what do you want to do?" She throws her hands in the air, her confidence in our plan clearly waning. "Either you go home now and face the music, which means your parents will probably put you in that shed thing again and definitely forbid you from seeing me. Which will also mean I'll have no way to get all of your clothes back to you. When they realize your clothes are gone, they'll probably figure out you weren't just coming over to hang out after school . . ."

She isn't wrong.

"So either we do this," she continues, "or you go home and things are a million times worse for you."

I recognize her street up ahead, a palm tree–lined slice of suburbia with stucco ranches painted in every hue from sunny yellow to pastel aquamarine to peachy-pink coral. It's a stark contrast from the beige-gray-brown I've lived with the last fifteen years.

"I can't go home," I say. "I can't go back there. We have to make this work, Rachel. *We have to.*"

"Okay." She stops, wrapping her hands around mine and capturing my gaze in hers. "Then we will."

I'm lying perfectly flat, perfectly still beneath a queen-sized bed in a room packed almost to the ceiling with cardboard boxes and plastic totes. My neck aches, and when I lift my head to change position, my hair catches on the underside of the mattress.

It's hard telling how long I've been in here.

Long enough to hear Mrs. Carmichael asking Rachel how her day went before reminding her to vacuum her room and put away the basket of clean clothes on her bed.

Long enough to hear Mr. Carmichael come home from work and drop his keys on the kitchen counter.

Long enough to hear the three of them debate about dinner before settling on take-out pizza.

Long enough to hear the doorbell ring when said pizza arrives and smell the savory scent coming from down the hall that makes my stomach rumble.

Long enough to contemplate the concerning fact that my parents haven't shown up here looking for me. Either Genevieve kept my secret (unlikely) or they're waiting for me to come home on my own so they can inflict a worse punishment than any I've ever known.

Since the Carmichaels are new to the church family and new to Cross Beach, I can't imagine my parents wanting to show up at their door unannounced asking if their daughter is here. It wouldn't look good for them, having such an errant, rebellious child. In fact, it would be embarrassing. It might show a crack in the perfect Fielding facade, and my father would sooner spend eternity in damnation than have his earthly reputation tarnished.

The natural light flooding this cramped room has faded from yellow to sunset orange to a plummy dusk before everything turns so dark I can't see my hand in front of my face.

I'm guessing it's at least nine thirty, which means the Carmichaels should be going to bed soon and I'll be able to finally leave.

Closing my eyes, I attempt to grab a little bit of rest before I make my midnight journey.

I'm awoken sometime later to the sound of swishing feet on the carpet and the quiet slide of cardboard boxes.

"Celia?" Rachel whispers. "It's time."

My tight muscles burn as I wiggle out of the cramped space, and she helps me up before placing a navy-blue duffel bag over my shoulder. Earlier she told me she stole it from her brother. Despite it being his favorite gym bag, she thought the color would act like a sort of camouflage in the night. I promised her I'd send it back when I got to where I was going and no longer needed it. She didn't seem concerned.

Lifting an index finger over her lips, she nods toward the window.

"My dad fell asleep in the living room," she says so softly I barely understand her. "You'll have to go out this way."

With quiet, careful deliberation, she slides the window open before popping out the screen, and then she crouches to the ground, cupping her hands to boost me up.

Standing on my toes, I unsling the duffel bag from my shoulder and slowly lower it to the ground outside. And then I step into her palms and hoist myself out. The fall to the other side is harder than I anticipated, and I land on my rear end after losing my footing.

"You okay?" she calls out, although in a whisper.

I nod.

With a hand over her heart, she looks at me with the saddest blue eyes I've ever seen and then sends me off with a silent wave.

Under the cover of darkness, I start the trek to the bus stop on the west side of town by the train tracks. But I don't make it more than half a block when a dark car parked on the opposite side of the street roars to life, blinding me with its headlights.

I lift my forearm to shield my vision, and I pick up my pace.

I was hoping I wouldn't be seen, but at least it's dark.

The driver's door opens with a slow creak before two heavy boots scuff the pavement.

"Celia." My father's voice is a low growl. "Get in the car. *Now.*"

I freeze, my shoes suddenly cemented to the sidewalk. Half of me wants to drop my bag and run—no, sprint—through the trees and bushes and backyards, knocking over trash cans as makeshift obstacles.

But my father is fit, and his long legs could move him faster than my young ones could ever move me. Besides, he loves a good foot chase. Everyone in the police department knows him as the one who never lets anyone get away. He is a skilled hunter, and I am unskilled prey.

"Celia." He says my name like he's forcing it through clenched teeth.

I turn to face him, shoulders slumped. I can't bring myself to look at him, to have that steely gaze seared into my memory forever.

"Get. In. The. Car." He opens the rear door of my mother's sedan. How I didn't recognize it when I walked by a second ago, I'm not sure. I suppose my mind was focused on other things . . . like leaving.

With no other options at hand, I follow his orders.

I slide into the back seat, though I don't buckle my seat belt. If we get hit by a train tonight, it just might be the best thing that could happen to me—a kinder fate than the one waiting for me at home, I'm sure.

"Your mother was worried sick when you failed to come home from school," he says when he takes his place behind the steering wheel. Before he shifts into drive, he adjusts the rearview mirror so he can watch me.

I cross my arms, feeling violated in a way. Exposed. Unearthed.

"Thank the good lord that Genevieve saw you with that Carmichael girl when she did or we'd have filed a missing person report," he says, shaking his head. "Last thing we need is to draw unnecessary attention to our family. Not to mention, sending out a search party for a teenage girl who simply ran away is a waste of law enforcement resources."

His lecture isn't as terse as it usually is, and his voice is eerily calmer than it should be given the circumstances. But I know from past experience, a calm-yet-angry Jim Fielding is a terrifying Jim Fielding.

A shiver routes through my entire body despite the back seat being stuffy and humid.

I can only imagine how long he was sitting there, stalking the Carmichael house, waiting for me to come out so he could apprehend me in a way that would draw the least amount of attention.

I bet he'd have waited all night long if he had to, and the large Styrofoam coffee cup in the center console agrees.

We pull into the driveway five excruciatingly silent minutes later.

He kills the engine, his eyes intersecting with mine in the rearview mirror before he steps out and gets the back door for me. My footsteps grow heavy the closer I get to the house, as if they know I'm marching closer to my questionable fate.

Hooking his hand on the back of my neck when we get inside, he steers me to my room.

"You're to stay in here all night, you understand? You don't leave for a drink of water or to use the bathroom, not once." He releases his grip on me and reaches for a drill on my nightstand. It's then that I realize he has screwed my window shut—something he's never done before.

I don't ask any questions, though, because at least he's not sending me to the hell shack for the night.

My father shoots me one last look before leaving. He pulls the door closed, and a second later, I hear his drill again, metal and wood clashing together like a symphony of strangeness.

Next, the snick of a dead bolt.

A dark shadow fills the space under the door, followed by the sound of him slumping against it.

Not only has he locked me in my room, but he's keeping watch all night to ensure I don't try to leave. It's ridiculous—the idea that I could escape something like this without someone in our small house hearing it. But I don't pretend to understand the way my father thinks. And I wouldn't want to. He's a terrifying person, and his mind would be an awful place to reside.

Crawling under my covers, I rest my cheek against my flattened pillow as thick tears slide down and dampen the case. Clamping my hand over my mouth, I silence my sobs. I know from experience that my father doesn't handle emotion well. It only tends to make things worse. He'll strike me until I cry, and then he'll strike me for crying.

Eventually sleep takes hold of me, and I welcome it with open arms. When I'm asleep, it's the only time I'm not here.

But my respite doesn't last long.

I'm yanked from my slumber with the smack of my bedroom door against the wall. Scrambling up, I press my back against the headboard as my father marches toward me. Behind him are two men dressed in black pants and T-shirts, their heads shaved. One of them reaches for his belt, retrieving a pair of handcuffs, while the other comes at me with his arms wide and hands splayed, as if I'm a wild animal he's about to catch.

A scream escapes my mouth, but my father silences it with a quick hand. I taste his salty palm as I kick, sending the bedspread to a crumpled pile on the floor while one of the men secures a cold metal handcuff on my wrist. The other man braces my ankles.

"Just stay calm now, Celia." My father's eyes are hollowed and dingy, as if he didn't sleep all night. "We don't want to upset your mother and sister."

He gives me an astute nod before slowly removing his hand from my mouth.

I gasp for air, fighting back tears that will only make this that much worse—if that's even possible.

"You're going to go away for a while." My father speaks as if I'm going off to summer camp—not that I'd know what that's like. But there's a haunting casualness in his tone that chills my core. "It pains us to do this, Celia, but you shouldn't have done what you did."

"What about what *you* did?" I clamp my own hand over my mouth. Did I really say that? Out loud?

He straightens his shoulders, his gaze icy and narrow.

I'm the only one who knows his secret—but even that isn't enough to outwit the most powerful man in my life. For the past year, I've kept it to myself, knowing that uttering those words to anyone would only make him call me a liar. That and he'd go on to ensure my life was one hundred times worse than it already was.

"I hope the good lord sees fit to send you back with a straighter head on those shoulders," he says before stepping out of the way. "I can't have you corrupting your sisters and disrespecting your mother and me. Your disobedience is no longer welcome in this house."

The men hook their arms under mine, their fingertips digging into my flesh, and drag me to the hallway. I pick up my feet, knowing resistance will only make this worse.

Once outside, they place me in the back of a gray van with grayed-out windows covered in some opaque film. The shorter of the two buckles me in before zip-tying my handcuffs to the seat belt. It isn't until we get moving a minute later that I realize there's another girl, whimpering, in the third row.

"Where are you taking us?" I ask. *"Where are you taking us?"*

My questions are met with silence.

I don't waste my energy again.

We drive for an eternity before pulling up to what appears to be a small campground encased by a wall of evergreens and a two-story fence topped in barbed wire. Small cabins are lined up along one side. A larger building rests across from them. A small sign at the entrance reads HEAVENLY SOLDIERS REFORMATORY. The driver scans a card at the gate, which swings open a moment later.

Up ahead, a group of teens jogs laps on a dirt path that encircles the cabin area, each one in matching gray sweats and a T-shirt emblazoned with a fiery cross and words too small for me to read from here.

One kid—who can't be much older than me—stops, hunches over, and loses the entire contents of his stomach. The clock on the dash read 7:12 AM when we arrived a minute ago. How long have they been running?

The driver parks next to the larger building, and the passenger climbs out, cutting my zip tie and helping me out with a rough pull of my arm, which causes me to lose my balance. I land on my hands and knees on dusty white gravel. The pointed shards of rock sting my palms.

"Whoops," the passenger says with a cruel chuckle.

I don't react—a skill I've mastered over the years.

"Come on, apologize, man. That wasn't right," the driver says, though his tone is mocking. I don't think for one second that he's sticking up for me.

"Nah. She needs to know who's running the show here," the passenger says. "The sooner she learns that, the better." He steps toward me, leaning in so close I can smell the coffee on his sour breath. "You're welcome."

The other girl in the van is hysterical.

"You going to get the other one, or you going to make me do that too?" the passenger says to his associate. He rolls his eyes and makes a move for the van before the other guy has a chance to respond. I stand back, watching powerlessly as he helps the poor thing out and then kicks the back of her knees. She falls to the ground in the same place I did, which I now realize has a decent-sized indentation. I don't want to think about how many others have met the same fate in that same place.

"Come on, girls. We don't have all day." The passenger points to the main doors of the large building. "Let's get you checked in so you don't miss out on your morning chores."

The inside of the building smells like the old, musty pull-behind camper we had when I was younger—when my family would go camping almost every weekend in the summertime. The change of scenery was always nice, but it never lasted long. By 6:00 AM Sunday morning, we were packing up and hauling back home in time for church.

"You must be Celia Fielding?" A thin woman with wide-set eyes and wavy brown hair glances up from a computer. "You're late."

"Traffic was insane on the—" one of the men begins to say, but she silences him with a lifted palm.

"Come with me." She waves for me to join her in the office before turning back to the other girl. "Sit tight. You'll be next."

I follow her beyond a door marked with a plaque that reads
BARBARA HOBBS, PROGRAM DIRECTOR. She takes a seat in a swivel chair
behind a neat and tidy desk, and then she motions for me to take the
one across from her.

"So." She gathers a long breath, looking me up and down, clasping
her hands together over her leather planner. "Your father tells me you've
been . . . *misguided* . . . lately."

"That's what he believes, ma'am, yes."

She lifts a palm, the way she did to the men who bullied me a
moment ago.

"I wasn't asking for your opinion, Celia," she says, enunciating each
syllable. "I was simply stating the reason why you're here. From now
on, you'll speak only when spoken to and only when I or one of your
superiors are asking a question. Please nod if you understand."

I swallow the hard lump in my throat, but it won't go down.

She lifts her brows, waiting for my nod—which I reluctantly give her.

The girl in the hall is crying louder now, sobbing, inconsolable.
One of the men tells her, "Your tears won't work here."

"I'm going to go over a few cursory details, Celia, and then you can
meet your supervising counselor and your bunkmates," she says. "Now,
I'm not sure if you've ever been to a summer camp before, but at our
camp we don't roast marshmallows; nor do we do arts and crafts. The
work we do is much more *involved* than that. We're going to save your
soul. Your parents sent you here as a last resort, and we take our job very
seriously. We're doing the lord's work in every sense of the word. Please
nod again if you understand."

I do as I'm told.

"When you leave here—whether it's next week, next month, or
next year—you're going to be a God-fearing, righteous young woman,
and your parents will be exceptionally proud of the work you've done."
She rises from her desk, perhaps a sign that her spiel is coming to a
close. "This isn't going to be easy for you. But just how hard it will be

will depend on you, Celia." I hate the way my name sounds on her lips . . . the subtle hint of disgust laced with condescension. "I won't sugarcoat this. Some of the worst days you'll ever have in your life will be here. But I can promise you, it'll be worth it. Life is full of rules and expectations. The sooner you accept that you're nothing more than a soldier of God, the sooner you can graduate from our program and lead the life you were always meant to live."

There was a boy at our church two summers ago who was always getting in trouble. But it was innocent fun. He liked to make people laugh, loved to get a reaction. He was silly more than anything else. Giving his brother bunny ears in the annual church photo. Drawing funny faces on the cartoon apostles on the Sunday school handouts. Doing the Macarena to "How Great Thou Art" and the sort of things that would often elicit giggles from other kids and stifled smiles from grown-ups who would immediately look guilty afterward.

Then one day he wasn't there anymore, but his parents were still coming to church. I overheard my parents talking about how he'd been sent away. By the time he came back that fall, something had changed. He was like a zombie—dead, distant eyes. Couldn't carry on a conversation . . . or maybe he wouldn't. Maybe he was scared. The poor thing looked shell-shocked, as if he'd been drafted to a war he hadn't wanted to fight and came back a changed person.

Wherever he went, whatever they did . . . it broke him.

I swallow the acidic burn of bile rising up the back of my throat as Barbara leads me to the door, and I stave off the tears that threaten to cloud my vision.

I won't let them break me.

CHAPTER 9

CELIA

Present day

I've been driving almost two hours when I end up at the parking lot for the Metro-North commuter train. It's a place I've been countless times before with Rob, as it's the route we always take for our weekends in Manhattan. But I've never been here this time of day—or rather, this time of morning. Aside from a handful of weekend travelers, the parking lot is mostly vacant except for the long-term parking section.

I pull into a spot, staring over my steering wheel toward the entrance and, beyond that, the station, where the 5:00 AM is coming to a stop at Platform 1. The sky fades from midnight blue to dark violet to peach as the sun rises in the east. A handful of cars pull in one by one, and I watch as Saturday-morning travelers make their way to the ticket counter inside. Some carry briefcases. Others carry nothing but a light jacket or a cell phone in hand. One woman tugs a large rolling suitcase behind her with an overstuffed weekend bag secured over the handle.

All these people are heading into the city, to their lives, to whoever is waiting for them on the other side of that bridge.

I'll bet none of them have ever received a cryptic note on their birthday.

A black car pulls up behind me, and the female driver immediately flips the visor down despite there being no sun shining in this direction, at least not yet. I watch her—the parts of her that I can see—in my side mirror. She slicks on lip balm, brushes her hair, applies a dot of hand cream.

I steer my gaze back on the station just in time to see the 5:00 AM train depart.

The restless ache still resides in my body, my anxiety simmering as it has been for hours now. Years ago, I saw a therapist who prescribed "naked walks"—walks where I didn't think about anything, didn't listen to anything. No podcasts. No music. Just the sights and sounds around me.

Perhaps it wouldn't hurt to walk around the city for a bit? Sometimes a change of scenery is enough to pull me out of an anxious spell. And goodness knows sitting in a car for another couple of hours won't do a damn bit of good.

I grab my bag, lock my car, and head inside to buy a round-trip ticket, shoving it in my pocket before heading to the platform to wait. I pull out my phone to check the time before tapping out a text to Rob to let him know where I am.

Out of an abundance of caution, I choose the car closest to the conductor—a little safety tip Monique Denman told me about. She's been accosted a time or two coming into the city to shop for antiques, and she said if you're traveling alone, it's always best to ride up front should anything happen. Not that I'm scared. But I don't have the added security of being with someone else.

I get settled into my seat and ready my ticket for the conductor. From the corner of my eye, I spot the woman from the black car trotting along the platform, heading this way. She opts for the train car behind me, leaving me by myself up here.

A minute later, I check my phone to see if Rob has texted back yet—only to find the message failed to send.

Weak signal. Go figure.

Leaning back, I watch the world outside my window, thinking about the last time we were here a month ago, celebrating our twenty-first wedding anniversary. Rob got us a table at the Lafayette Supper Club as well as front-row tickets to *Funny Girl* on Broadway. We spent Friday night wining and dining and Saturday morning ambling city sidewalk sales and pop-up farmers markets before catching our matinee. When we returned to our hotel that evening, Rob had an in-room couples massage waiting for us.

The train stops at Grand Central Station, where I transfer to a subway and ride it all the way to Christopher Street, partly because there's something calming about the gentle lull of the tracks but also because I'm not quite sure where I want to go yet. I figured I'd start at the bottom, work my way uptown, and grab a ride back in the early afternoon.

The city is alive by the time I merge with the rest of civilization. Locals and tourists carrying coffees, chatting at outdoor cafés over powdered sugar crepes and poached eggs, snapping photos and hailing taxis.

Life is all around me—effervescent and bustling.

I tuck my messy bedhead under my cap, slip on a pair of sunglasses to hide my tired eyes, and trek up the street. With every city block, the chattering in my mind about that stupid letter becomes background noise. When I go home, it'll still be there, waiting for me on the dining room table where I left it, but at least here I'll get a brief reprieve.

I wander for a solid hour and a half, choosing side streets at random and stopping to admire window displays whenever they catch my eye. To be honest, I have no idea which neighborhood I'm in now. Nothing here is familiar, and I'm passing row upon row of nightclubs and basement bars.

Up ahead is an empty bus bench, so I take a seat and pull out my phone—which is now dead.

"Shoot," I say.

I've never been one of those people who treats their phone as a life-sustaining necessity, which means I've never worried about my battery dying or lugged around a spare battery bank or charger, because it's always fully charged. But I took a lot of pictures and videos last night, and my phone was blowing up with happy birthday texts the entire day.

I gather in a lungful of stale city air and sink back against the bench as the heaviness of sheer exhaustion blankets over me for the first time in days.

Just thinking about the jaunt back home feels like I'm approaching the starting line of the New York City Marathon.

I need to call Rob and make sure he knows I'm okay. He isn't one to worry or assume the worst—which is one of the things I've always admired about him. In fact, knowing him, he'll wake up sometime around nine, find my note, and assume I'm off running errands. He'll drink his coffee, turn on some morning golf, and peruse the *Wall Street Journal* for a bit. By the time I get home today, he won't have broken a sweat missing me.

Peeling myself off the bench, I trudge to the next street corner. Up ahead is a man with a Yankees jacket on, laughing into his phone. For a second, I consider asking him if I could use it to make a call . . . but then I think about all the times I've been approached by strangers at gas stations or malls asking for the same thing. It's such a strange request in a day and age when everyone has a phone. Rob told me it's usually some kind of scam, a way to distract you so they can do whatever they're trying to do—steal your wallet, run off with your phone, anything.

I make it two more blocks in search of a bodega where I can buy a power bank and charger . . . only to find a doughnut shop with a line literally out the door and around the corner.

Another block later, I pass a crumbling hotel with a lit VACANCY sign in the window. Fatigue gnawing at my insides like a starving dog with a bone, I head inside.

"Hi, excuse me," I say to the young lady working the front desk. She peers up at me through mile-long lashes and doesn't attempt to hide her annoyance at my presence. "I'm so sorry to bother you, but could I use your phone to call my husband?"

Her deathlike gaze drips over me from head to toe and back before she cocks her head to the side.

"What does this look like to you, a Verizon?" She rolls her eyes and makes a shooing motion toward the door.

Heat creeps up my neck. I've never been spoken to like that before . . . at least not in my adult life. But I clear my throat and stay determined to keep on the high road.

"I know it's an inconvenience, but my phone is dead. The bodega down the street is temporarily closed. I don't want to keep wandering around looking for another one." I make my voice sweet and keep my demeanor calm and pleasant.

"Sounds like a personal problem." She doesn't blink.

"You're right. It is." I smile.

"So what do you want me to do about it, lady?" Her name tag identifies her simply as Cash.

"I'd be so grateful if I could just use your phone for . . . thirty seconds," I say. "Just long enough to let my husband know I'm on my way home." Digging into my bag, I produce my lifeless cell phone and show her the black screen.

"I'm sorry, but who walks around with a dead phone in this day and age?" She sniffs an amused laugh.

"Apparently I do." I soften my voice and my gaze and hope she can see that I'm only human.

She doesn't owe me anything, my problem isn't hers, and I'm just some woman who looks like she rolled out of bed and wandered in here . . . which is essentially what I did. I don't blame her for not wanting to give me the time of day. I imagine various types of people meander in here all the time bothering her.

"I'll tell you what," I say, keeping pleasant. "Why don't I rent a room . . . and then I'll go into that room and use that phone and then check out?"

Her lips twist at the side as she raps her neon-green, jewel-encrusted fingernails on the counter.

"We don't start check-in until three," she says.

"Then I'll pay for last night's rate."

"My system won't let me do that," she says, "and even if it would, the system's down. I can't take your credit card. I can't even make a phone call because the genius owner of this place got our phone service through some cheap satellite internet company."

I yawn, resting my elbow against the tall countertop and placing my forehead against my palm. There's got to be a way to do this.

"When do you think your system will be up and running?" I ask, my eyelids growing heavier by the second. To be honest, a power nap would be incredible right now.

"Your guess is as good as mine. The company said they'd send a technician between eight and noon. I'm sure you know how that goes . . ."

"All right." I scan the wall of keys behind her, counting three available rooms out of ten. This is a small establishment, where rules can be bent if not broken, I imagine. "What's your nightly rate?"

"One fifty with taxes."

"I'll pay you last night's rate and tonight's rate . . . cash . . . if you get me one of your rooms to hang out in while we wait for your internet guy to show up."

Before she has a chance to respond, I've already dug into my wallet and pulled out three crisp hundred-dollar bills. Sensing hesitation, I add one more. A tip of sorts.

"Ma'am—"

"Please," I say. "I haven't slept in two days. I just want to take a nap and call my husband. That's all I want to do. My cell is dead. I'm exhausted. I have no idea where I am. I just need a place to rest."

I lower my forehead to the top of the counter, knowing full well I could fall asleep right here with this slab of granite as my pillow.

But then I hear the clink of keys beside my ear.

"Fine. I'll put you in eight." Cash grabs the money. "But you have to be out of here by tomorrow no matter what. We're booked solid the night after."

"Thank you. Thank you so much. I'll be gone before then." For a moment, I debate asking if she has a spare phone charger, but I get the sense I shouldn't press my luck. "Can you let me know when the phones are working?"

"Yeah, I'll have our *concierge* get right on that." She winks. "Or you could, you know, just lift the receiver, press nine, and see if you get a dial tone?"

"That works," I say as she inspects the bills. "Thanks again. I really appreciate it."

Cash says nothing; she simply sends me away with a look that suggests I better not get her in trouble.

I follow the signs to room eight, a small, fusty room with a single queen-sized bed and the stale scent of marijuana lingering in the air.

But a bed is a bed.

I collapse on top of the brown covers and let sleep sink her heavy teeth into the deepest parts of me.

CHAPTER 10

Genevieve

Twenty-five years ago

I pass my sister's room in the morning only to find her door wide open and her bed empty. I saw her walking home with the Carmichael girl after school yesterday, but I assumed she'd be home soon enough, so I kept my mouth shut.

But dinnertime came and went, as did bath time and bedtime, and my parents were pacing the house, worried sick. I overheard my father telling my mother about some guy he just arrested who was trying to kidnap a girl from Cimarron Park, as well as some new gang causing all sorts of trouble in the next town over, and then I watched as he grabbed his off-duty weapon and the car keys and said he was tired of sitting around waiting for her to come home.

With my heart in my teeth, I stopped him on the way to the back door . . . and told him what I saw.

I didn't want to betray my sister, but I also didn't want her kidnapped.

My father's eyes turned stormy, and he muttered something under his breath before slamming the door behind him and peeling out of the driveway.

There was no denying Celia had something coming—but whatever penance she'll have to pay has to be better than winding up dead in some ditch.

I leave her room and make a beeline for the living room, praying she's hanging out by the bay window with her nose stuck in a book like it's any other morning. Only she isn't there either. I check the hall bath next, followed by the kitchen, where Mom is making breakfast, humming the same haunting hymn that played at my grandmother's funeral last year. My father flips through the newspaper, completely oblivious to my presence, which is nothing new.

I'm used to being the wallpaper of the family anyway: rarely seen and seldom heard unless someone needs something.

"Where's Celia?" I ask.

My mother stops humming.

My father lowers his paper before sliding his reading glasses off his nose and placing them aside. My mother shoots him a look that makes my stomach sink.

"You found her last night, right?" I ask before they can answer, because I can't stand another second of unsettling silence.

"We did," my father says.

I exhale, relief flooding my veins.

"Thanks to you," he adds. "You did the right thing coming to me last night. Turns out she was at the Carmichaels' the whole time."

"Where is she now?" I ask.

"She isn't here." He clears his throat, gazing past my shoulder before focusing his eyes on me again.

I release a nervous laugh, confused. "Okay . . . so where is she?"

"Your sister," he says with the soothing composure of a seasoned prayer leader, "is going away for a while."

I grip the back of a kitchen chair, steadying myself. There was a boy from church a while back who was sent away. I don't know where they sent him. I just remember he was gone a very long time, and when he came back, he was different. Like the light in his eyes had been extinguished. Celia noticed it first. It was more upsetting to her than it was to me, but they were closer in age and had classes together. Time and time again after he'd returned, she would talk about the old him as if that version were dead and someone completely new had taken his place.

"Wh-where?" I manage to ask. "Where'd she go?"

"She's gone to get right with the lord," Mom answers.

"How long will she be gone?" I'm not sure I want to know, but I ask anyway.

"However long it takes." Dad adjusts his reading glasses and straightens the newspaper.

I think of Celia's stubborn streak.

"Can I . . . send her letters? Call her?" I ask.

I don't care if she's been distant lately; I already feel her absence in my bones. Hollow and deep. Unsettling. It's like someone sawed off an appendage and now I'm going to have to adjust to life without it. Already her void feels unnatural.

"No," he says. "It's against protocol. She needs to be fully immersed in the program. No distractions."

The room begins to spin, and the humid breakfast-scented air around me churns my stomach.

"I can see you're upset, Genevieve," my father says. "Why don't you take a seat and get some food in you so you can go about the rest of your day?"

How could I eat at a time like this? When my sister has been ripped from my life with no warning and cut off from all communication?

"Take a deep breath now." The warmth of my mom's hands on my shoulders pulls me out of my head, but the heat of anger still burns beneath my skin. Only it isn't my parents I'm angry with—it's Celia.

She did this.

She brought this upon herself.

She brought this upon *all* of us.

"You did the right thing," Mom says. "If it weren't for you, who knows what would've happened to your sister last night?"

My father reaches for his coffee, tilting it toward me. "Your mother is right. You just might've saved Celia's life. Her soul, too."

If I did the right thing . . . why does it feel so wrong?

CHAPTER 11

C ELIA

Twenty-four years ago

"I have to say, Mr. and Mrs. Fielding, I'm quite impressed with Celia's progress at the reformatory. It was a little bumpy at first, but we ironed out those kinks, and I'm so pleased to be sitting here with you all today to share what a dedicated and righteous young lady she's become." Barbara Hobbs chose to personally deliver me to my parents today, for reasons I don't quite understand. Apparently she never does this. It's usually a delegated counselor or someone one level beneath her.

She reaches over, placing her hand on my shoulder and giving me a warm smile, the kind I never once saw in the entire year I spent under her devout dictatorship.

My parents look exactly the way they did a year ago.

They can't say the same for me, though. The clothes they sent for me to wear are hanging off my frame, and I saw the way Genevieve looked at me when she saw me come in—you'd have thought she'd seen a ghost. They didn't allow mirrors there—safety reasons, I guess—but I can only imagine the gaunt shadows casting across my face, and I don't have to see my eyes to feel how they've sunken into my skull.

The food there was dreadful . . . "gray sludge," we called it. The counselors called it "mush," and they'd laugh and crumple their McDonald's wrappers while we picked around at our plates. I overheard one say that she tried to feed it to her dog as an experiment and her dog pushed the bowl away.

When we weren't wasting away on a diet of slop and slurry, we were running laps around the grounds—five miles' worth a day, per my calculations. We had our devotions and our chores to fill the rest of the gaps. I wish I could say the time went by in the blink of an eye, but every minute there felt like an hour in the outside world.

"I'm delighted to share with you that Celia took on a bit of a leadership role in our community over the past six months," Barbara continues. "Our very first Heavenly Soldiers mentor."

She makes it sound pleasant and uplifting when it was anything but.

All I did was teach the newcomers how to survive there, how to act the part. I told them if they played victim or cried or begged for anything at all, they'd only get it ten times worse. My *mentor* program was so successful that almost all my *mentees* left the facility long before I did. I imagine they were only holding on to me for their own benefit, because I made their program look successful, which only got them more referrals.

But while these monsters wanted to break us down and reconstruct us into shells of ourselves, I showed the new kids how to stay strong.

Barbara finishes her spiel, which sounds like more of a sales pitch than anything else, before my parents walk her to the door.

"Please, if you know of anyone else needing our services, don't hesitate to give them my name. We're all doing the lord's work, and one child saved is . . ." she rambles from the next room. I tune her out, praying I never have to hear that wretched fake voice again.

As soon as the front door closes, the house fills with deafening silence.

I wait at the table for my parents to return. I suppose I'm still used to being told when I can leave and where I'm permitted to go at all times.

"I'm proud of you, Celia." My father's voice cuts through the room. I swivel around and find him standing in the doorway, his hands over my mother's shoulders. She's yet to show an ounce of a reaction since my return, not that I had expectations. Part of me had hoped that maybe, just *maybe*, she'd missed me. Her daughter. Her firstborn. Her flesh and blood.

One of the biggest components of the program is the requirement that all communication between parent and child be cut off. The counselors and Barbara were the only ones allowed to relay messages either way. They said it was for the benefit of the children, that it helped them settle in quicker. They claimed that talking to our parents would only make us homesick.

Not once did I miss the sound of my parents' voices, but I did miss my home. Being sent away to Heavenly Soldiers was like graduating to another circle of hell.

But I watched as other kids struggled with not being able to call home or hear a familiar voice. Many of them would sob themselves to sleep those first weeks, feeling abandoned and discarded. The counselors would comfort them with words like, "This is your home. We're your family now." But they'd do it with a wicked gleam in their eye, as if their comfort were nothing more than mockery in disguise.

"It wasn't easy for us, you know," my mother says. "We were backed into a corner. We saw you veering off onto the wrong path, and we had to take action as soon as possible. We had to save your soul."

Her eyes widen, but her expression is still that of a woman who's been dead inside for decades. She's nothing but a puppet echoing my father's sentiments and a vessel to bring his children into this world.

There's no love when she looks at me; there's no warmth in her voice.

Maybe there never was and it took the past year for me to see it.

My lower lip trembles, but I manage to fight it off.

"Thank you." I say the words they taught us to say—they all but beat gratitude into us. "You saved my soul, and for that I'll be forever grateful."

Mom's lips curl into a tight smile, and she pats my father's hands, which are still anchored onto the tops of her narrow shoulders.

"That's my girl," my father says, motioning for me to come closer.

I rise from the table, make my way across the room, and accept the rare hug he's offering. He pulls me close, tight underneath one arm, squeezing me so hard it forces the air from my lungs. Next he kisses the top of my head.

"Proud of you," he says.

"May I be excused to go to my room?" I ask. "It's time for my morning devotions."

My mother tilts her head, exhaling with a pleased glint in her eyes as she looks up at my father.

"Of course, Celia," he answers.

I pass Genevieve in the hallway, standing there with wide doe eyes, our squirming two-year-old sister on her hip. My shoulder brushes against hers and not by accident.

For twelve months I've thought about all the things I'd say to Genevieve when I saw her again. But my satisfaction would be short lived because the girl is a rat.

She'd tell on me in a heartbeat.

I'd be back in that horrid place by tomorrow, and I'd rather die than spend another night there again.

In two years, I'll be an adult.

In two years, I'll leave again—this time for good.

CHAPTER 12

Celia

Present day

I wake with a start in a room as suffocatingly humid as the hell shack my father used to lock me in. Gasping for air, I startle with a kick before sinking back into my sweat-damp pillow once the air conditioner kicks on.

The other side of the bed is cold and empty, and my mind goes to Rob. Reaching for the phone on the nightstand, I lift the receiver to my ear, press the number nine button, and wait for a dial tone that never comes.

I press zero for the hell of it, a feeble attempt to reach the front desk, but I get nothing but dead air.

The blinding red letters on the alarm clock read 8:05, but I'm not sure if it's AM or PM. Either way, I haven't felt this rested in ages. Whether I slept for ten hours or twenty-two, my body certainly needed it.

I peel myself off the bed, place my arms out to feel for the wall, and navigate to the small en suite bathroom. Flicking on the light, I squint until my eyes adjust, and then I splash some cool water on my face, finger comb my hair into place, and slip my shoes on to head out to find a phone charger so I can call my husband and tell him I'm safe.

CHAPTER 13

CELIA

Twenty-two years ago

I drag my red pen across today's date on my desktop calendar. In less than three months, I'll be in college—no longer a prisoner under my parents' roof and one step closer to true freedom. For now, I'm working part time at a local accounting firm, saving pennies and biding time.

The front door swings open, and my boss's son strolls in, ushering in a burst of summer heat. In one smooth move, he slides his black Wayfarers off his nose and rests them on top of his head before giving everyone a friendly wave and making a beeline for his father's office with two brown paper bags in tow.

I try not to stare . . . key word being "try."

When Rob Guest is here, it takes everything I have not to lose my focus on my filing.

"Celia, you all right?" The other summer temp nudges my shoulder before handing me another pile of unalphabetized folders. "You seem a little . . . distracted."

"Sorry." I accept the pile and redirect my gaze. "Must've been lost in thought."

From what the other girls here have said, I've pieced together that he's thirty-one, single, and runs a local nursing home. Someone mentioned his parents are desperate for him to get married and settle down, but he claims he hasn't met the right person yet. People here like to speculate all kinds of things, but I've never liked to make assumptions about people without knowing them. It isn't kind.

"Mm-hmm," she says, her attention passing from me to Rob Guest and back. A second later, she chuckles before fanning her face. "It's definitely hot in here, and it isn't because it's the middle of July . . ."

I don't react. I'm not supposed to. And I shouldn't. I have no business entertaining crushes, especially when they involve my boss's thirty-one-year-old son, who just so happens to stop in twice a week to have lunch with his dad. Occasionally he'll wander around the office making small talk. Sometimes he'll bring doughnuts. Other times he'll bring flowers. He never forgets a name or a birth date or some random tidbit of information from a twenty-second conversation he had weeks back.

Mona McNabb calls him "Prince Charming" whenever the boss is out of earshot. And then she says, "If I were just twenty years younger . . ."

I mean, she's not wrong.

Those soft, olive-green eyes and that fringe of dark lashes . . . his broad shoulders . . . those chocolate waves that I can only imagine would feel like silk between my fingers. And his dimples. Don't get me started on those.

I'd be lying if I said he didn't make me think the kind of thoughts that are far too mature for my eighteen years.

From my periphery, I see him disappear into his father's office, and I release a tight breath. Every time he comes in here, my body gets all heated and fidgety, like it's malfunctioning. Like it's hyperaware. That's the only way I can describe it.

"I'm going to take my break," I tell the other temp before resting the stack of files on top of the cabinet. "Be back in fifteen."

I head to the break room to grab my Diet Coke from the fridge, then step outside and take a seat at the picnic table under the shade tree. The mid-July air is thick and soupy, but the sunshine feels nice against my air-conditioned skin. Mr. Guest keeps the office at a cool sixty-eight degrees. Mona always complains about having to "work in an icebox," but I imagine it could be worse. Some people have to work outside in this weather. Or in costumes, like at Disney World. I'm not sure how they don't feel suffocated when it's a hundred degrees out and they're trapped in some thick getup with a giant cartoon character head.

The back door opens, and I glance over to see who's interrupting my fifteen minutes of solitude—the only time I'm truly alone these days.

I almost choke on my spit when I see who it is.

"Hey there." Rob Guest trots down the steps, stopping at the bottom. "Celia, right?"

My fingertips are frozen against my sweaty Coke can. I nod. "Yep."

"My father said you're thinking about going to Cross Beach College." He scratches at his temple, studying me.

My lips part, but nothing comes out. Not at first. My parents enrolled me for the fall without asking me. While CBC is a private institution, the Church of True Believers is its largest benefactor. Almost all the deans, professors, and advisers are members of the church, which means the curriculums are . . . *tailored*. People from sister congregations all over the country send their kids here to be educated—or rather, further indoctrinated. With a student body of nearly five thousand and growing yearly, it's become quite the machine.

Rob slides his hands in his pockets, coming closer. "I went there. Many moons ago. That's why I was asking."

I straighten my slumped shoulders, suddenly hyperaware of my posture, and I resist the urge to fix the wayward strand of hair grazing my left cheek.

"That's the plan," I say, leaving out the part about me ditching town as soon as I get there. I've been saving money all summer—a couple thousand dollars so far after taxes—and I should have a couple thousand more by then. Once I'm moved into my dorm this September and get my student-loan money, I'll pack my bags and get out of here. Now that I'm eighteen, they can't stop me. And with me being away at school, despite it being a mere five miles from our house, they won't know that I've left until it's too late.

"My parents made me go there," he said. "Hated every second of it. But they were paying, so . . . free college, I guess?"

His button-down shirt is cuffed just below his elbows, and something catches my eye.

A tattoo.

Rob's father is one of the deacons at our church—it's how I got this summer job. His father is much like mine: devout, disciplined, obsessed with righteousness. Only his father seems genuine. At least from what I can tell. He's kind, never raises his voice, and he certainly never gets that wild look in his eyes that my father gets from time to time.

My stare is fixated on the black inscription on Rob's inner forearm. It's not that I've never seen a tattoo before . . . I've just never seen one on someone like *us*.

"Oh, this?" He slides his hand out of his pocket and angles the inside of his arm so his ink is on full display. "You like it?"

"I'm just . . . how did you . . . did your parents . . ." When I realize what it is—an upside-down cross, black on one side, white on the other, and a gray line separating the two—I can't form a complete sentence.

Rob chuckles, his dimples flanking his bright white grin. "Got it the day I graduated from college. You know, it's funny. My parents sent me there thinking I'd become even more like them, but all it did was open my eyes. Nothing is black and white. No one has a monopoly on the truth."

"Your parents didn't disown you?" I don't want to think about what my parents would do if I branded my body with rebellion.

He sniffs, his smile fading. "My mother cried. For days. My father wouldn't speak to me for a solid month. But eventually they forgave me. That's the godly thing to do, right?"

"So . . . just like that? Water under the bridge?"

He nods. "More or less, yeah."

I lean my elbow against the picnic table and rest my chin on the top of my hand. My parents have never forgiven me for anything. They simply punish and move on.

"Anyway, CBC is a good school," he says. "Academically, I mean. What are you studying?"

"I haven't picked a major yet. My parents signed me up without asking."

He winces. "That's tough."

"Your tattoo," I say, eyeing the ink once again. "Do you still believe those things? About nothing being black and white?"

His dark brows rise. "One million percent, yeah. Everything has a gray area."

He traces the gray line that divides the black and white sides of the cross.

"Why is the cross upside down?" I ask.

"Depends on who you ask," he says. "Some people say it stands for martyrdom. Other people say it stands for devil worshipping."

"What does it mean to you?"

Rob pauses, raking his hand along his sharp jaw and gazing at the concrete. "Wasn't expecting to get this deep on a Tuesday afternoon with someone I hardly know, but . . ." He laughs through his nose. "I guess, to me, it stands for everything I learned being turned upside down."

"Wow."

"I'm sorry. I know you go to my dad's church and you're a *believer* and all of that. I don't want to corrupt your mind with my philosophical take on organized Pentecostal religion or anything." He winces. "My father would kill me. Not literally, of course. But he wouldn't be too pleased if I led you astray . . ."

"So you left the church," I say.

He chuffs. "A lifetime ago, yes."

"And your parents are okay with that?"

"They're one hundred percent convinced I'm going straight to hell when I die," he says with a smirk. "But they'd never write me off. They're not like that. We just don't discuss religion anymore. Anything but."

Religion is the only thing we discuss in my family.

"Anyway, please don't let anything I said deter you from doing what you planned to do with your life." He places a splayed palm over his chest. "It's not my place to tell anyone who or what to believe."

The stir of *something* whirs inside me, pattering inside my rib cage like a butterfly trying to escape.

"I should get going," he says, jangling his keys. "Good talking with you, though, Celia."

The way he says my name makes me forget we're a hair beyond strangers and sends my heart into a full gallop.

"See you, Rob." I say his name out loud for the first time, and it makes my mouth tingle.

The sun beats down with an invigorated intensity as I watch him climb into his black Hyundai coupe and exit the parking lot. While all the other ladies in the office look at him and see a handsome, charismatic bachelor, I now see him for what he truly is: a freethinking rebel.

I finish my Diet Coke and head inside.

And I think about Rob Guest the rest of the day.

All evening, too.

Something tells me he was made for me. Or I was made for him. I feel it—I know it—in the deepest part of my soul. And when I lay my head on my pillow at the end of the night, I pray to a God that owes me no favors, begging that he'll someday make Rob mine.

Surely after everything I've been through, after all the penance I've done, he'll give me this one thing?

CHAPTER 14

Genevieve

Twenty-two years ago

I watch from the kitchen window as Celia climbs into her car, untwists her braids until they form cascading waves down her shoulders, and then slicks on a coat of pink lip balm. Ever since she started working at Guest Accounting Services, she's changed. When she's not loitering in front of the bathroom mirror and taking her sweet time getting ready, she's humming songs I've never heard before and walking around with her head in the clouds.

This fall she's going off to college, and I worry the wedge that has already divided us these last few years will only grow deeper.

Ever since she returned from the reformation camp, she hasn't wanted much to do with me. In her eyes I'm nothing but a rat. She doesn't understand that I did what I did because I feared for her safety . . . because she's my sister . . . because I love her . . . because if anything had happened to her that night, I would never have been able to live with myself.

I keep hoping that one day she'll wake up and forgive me. That she'll rap on my door and ask if I want to play a game of cards on the patio or help her make fresh lemonade like we used to every summer.

But with each passing day, memories of the sister I knew grow more distant.

I'm not sure if the old Celia will ever come back. It's almost like she's dead and gone, replaced by a stranger.

My parents have always tried to make an example out of Celia so that Celeste and I don't fall down the wrong path like she did. But they no longer have to worry because I don't want to be anything like her anyway.

I walk away from the window as Celia backs out of the driveway, and I head to Celeste's room to get her ready for the day. While I secure her pigtails with two pink elastics and matching bows, I make a silent promise to her.

No matter what happens, I'll never leave her behind.

I'll never be that kind of sister.

CHAPTER 15

CELIA

Present day

I leave the bodega, charger in hand, and trek back to the hotel. The woman in line behind me a few minutes ago was on the phone with someone, talking about dinner reservations, so it must be evening. The streets are still as empty as they were this morning, though given the fact that it's a Saturday and these blocks are lined with dive bars and dance clubs, that should all change soon enough.

It's three blocks back to the hotel, and I can't get there fast enough. Rob must be worried sick. I imagine he's tried to reach me a hundred times by now, and the instant my phone has a single volt of juice, I'll call him.

Warmth floods my veins at the thought of hearing his voice again. It's always been a comfort to me, a balm to my soul.

When we first began dating, sometimes I'd ask him to read out loud to me, just so I could hear him talk. I'd close my eyes and listen to the way he enunciated with such confidence, the way his emotions would curl around the words and practically bring them to life. I always told him he had a voice for radio and a face for TV, but that sort of thing has never mattered to him. He's never wanted attention or adoration from anyone but me.

I round the first corner just in time to catch a streetlight burn out, though it doesn't encapsulate everything in darkness. Up ahead is a dark alley. An electric, unsettled sensation passes through me. I trot ahead, passing the backstreet as quickly as I can.

At the end of the block, I get caught at a crosswalk with a flashing orange sign forbidding me from stepping off the curb. Despite there being no cars and no people, I remain anchored to the cement, waiting for the sign to change. Twenty-plus years ago, I was an astute rule follower. While I've tried to free my spirit since then, I've accepted the fact that some rules are in place for safety reasons.

A minute passes, maybe longer, and I start to feel ridiculous, standing here at this empty corner, waiting to cross a vacant street.

The light flashes with permission to walk the instant I take my first step into the faded lines of the intersection.

"Figures," I say under my breath.

I'm a block from my hotel when something—someone—strikes me on the back of the head. I turn around to confront the jerk, only to be met with another blow before I get a chance to see their face.

I fall to the ground as a shock of pain roars through my head and my vision fades in and out.

All I catch is a blur of darkness.

Dark hat, dark clothes, a face covered in a dark ski mask.

My attacker yanks my purse off my shoulder, tugging so hard they nearly pull my arm from the socket. I attempt to grab it back, but it's no use. They take off sprinting, my phone, purse, car keys—everything I have right now—in their possession.

I scream for help, my voice echoing off the brick facades that flank this alley.

I crawl toward a nearby dumpster, grab on, and push myself to standing. Only the moment I'm upright, the pulsing throbs in my head turn violent, and the world around dizzies before fading out altogether.

CHAPTER 16

CELIA

Twenty-two years ago

I climb into the passenger side of Rob's car. He pulls me in for a kiss before I get a chance to shut the door. His lips against mine and his hand cradling the back of my neck bring me to life.

For the past six weeks, I've been taking every Tuesday and Friday afternoon off work to spend with Rob. My parents would quite literally kill me if they knew what I was doing. And Rob hasn't mentioned anything to his father either, opting to leave him out of the equation because he surely wouldn't approve of this.

After Rob told me the meaning of his tattoo, I pulled him aside the next time I saw him and continued the conversation. I picked his fascinating brain, loading up on the kinds of theories and beliefs I wouldn't dream of uttering in a million years. But our little fifteen-minute conversations here and there were hardly enough to fill my empty cup.

I wanted more of him.

I wanted *all* of him.

I wanted Rob Guest in a way I've never wanted anything or anyone in my entire life.

During one of our early conversations, he told me about the idea of ask, believe, and receive, and how we can shape our realities with our minds. I'd never heard anything like it before, but I gave it a try. Every night for weeks, I asked God . . . the universe . . . whoever was listening . . . to bring Rob and me together. Then I believed it would happen with all my heart.

Three weeks later, he kissed me for the first time.

Now here we are, living for these stolen afternoons when we sit and talk for hours in his car, a world away from everything else. No one to bother us. No one to judge us. No one to make us feel guilty or shameful.

The hours that exist outside this bubble are meaningless. I might as well be dead. But when we're together, when I'm the object of his affection, I come alive, unfolding like a flower in springtime.

"You taste like cinnamon," I tell him, running my fingers through his silky hair and inhaling his faded woodsy aftershave.

"You taste like everything that's right in this world." He steals another kiss.

Before all this, I told him about my childhood. About my parents' extreme expectations and punishments. I told him about being sent away for a year and everything I did to survive. I told him I'd been questioning this religion for as long as I can remember and that when I saw his tattoo, I felt like I'd found someone like me for the first time in my life.

Rob was horrified. He said the Church of True Believers is extreme compared to many other Pentecostal offshoots, but he assured me most of them weren't half as brutal as my parents.

When I told him my plan to leave, he was nothing but supportive, offering to do whatever he could to help.

But leaving Cross Beach means leaving Rob, too.

"You should come with me," I tell him.

"What?"

"When I leave next month." I hold my gaze on his, silently pleading with him to join me.

Ask . . . believe . . . receive . . .

He leans back into his chair, lifting a hand across his forehead, temple to temple, as he exhales.

"I can't stay here, Rob," I say.

"I know."

"But I don't want to leave you." My heart races so hard it pulsates in my ears. Despite the AC running at full blast, the air in here now feels stifled and suffocated. Is he having second thoughts about me? About us? Is he just going to let me go? After everything?

"I can't just quit my job," he says, "without having another one lined up."

"You can find another job, right? There are nursing homes all over the country. Surely one of them somewhere is looking for a new administrator. You're educated and you have experience. And everybody likes you the instant they meet you . . ."

He exhales, his expression too humble for his own good. "I don't know about *that*."

I roll my eyes. Now is not the time for him to be modest, not when our future is at stake.

"I have a few thousand dollars saved up, and I'll be getting another five grand when my student loans go through next month," I say. Surely he has savings as well, though it's not something we've ever discussed. I've never pried into his financial business because I'm not that kind of person and this is still so new. "That can buy us some time to figure things out?"

He rests his elbow against the driver's-side door and stares beyond the steering wheel, into the empty parking lot of an abandoned Piggly Wiggly on the south side of town.

"I'll be honest, Celia. I wasn't expecting to like you as much as I do," he says. I draw in a long breath and hold it tight in my chest as I wait for him to qualify his confession with words that will likely break my heart. "I also wasn't expecting this to happen."

He motions between the two of us, his heart to mine and back.

I collect myself, but only a little. I still feel like I'm dangling over a cliff, about to be dropped at any moment.

"A lot of folks might not be happy about us being together," he says. "I'm thirteen years older than you." He sniffs. "Two months ago you were still in high school. I'm not going to sugarcoat how wrong that would seem to someone who doesn't understand what we have."

"So now you're worried about what people who don't know us would think about us?" My brows meet. "I guess I'm confused because you gave me the impression that you don't care what anyone thinks of you . . ."

"I don't care what people think about me when it comes to my personal beliefs. But a thirty-one-year-old man running away with an eighteen-year-old woman." He winces. "God, just saying it out loud . . . it feels wrong." He turns his attention to me. "But when I look at you, when I'm with you, when we're talking . . . it just feels right."

"So you're having second thoughts."

"I'm conflicted," he says without mincing words. "I want to be with you, Celia. But I don't think I should be."

Thick tears obscure my vision. I swipe them away the second they fall.

I asked, I believed, I received. And now God, the universe—whoever—is taking him away.

"You deserve better than what you've been through," he adds. "You're young, Celia. You're a bit naive. I don't want you to wake up twenty years from now and feel like I took advantage of that."

"If you don't want to be together, just say that." I dab the back of my hand against my wet cheek.

"I want to be with you."

"But?"

"But it's complicated."

"What was your end goal with all of this? What did you think was going to happen when we started spending time together?"

He presses his lips flat. "I had no idea. I just knew that I looked forward to seeing you. I just knew there was a connection. And the more I tried to fight my feelings, the stronger they'd become. I guess I wasn't thinking long term."

I don't tell him I've already mentally mapped out the rest of my life with him, building an entire fictional future around a man who I believed was my soul mate.

"People have taken advantage of your innocence your entire life, Celia," he says. "I don't want to be another name on that list."

"I'm not as innocent as you think."

He squints, as if he doesn't follow. And he wouldn't. While I've told him nearly everything there is to know about me, there was one detail I intentionally left out. I couldn't bring myself to tell him what happened the summer I turned fourteen.

That's something I can't tell anyone—something I'm taking to the grave.

CHAPTER 17

GENEVIEVE

Present day

"Genevieve?" My sister's husband calls me Saturday morning. "It's Rob."

The number of times this man has called me in the twenty-plus years they've been married, I could count on one hand, which is why I decided to answer.

"What's up?" My voice is groggy and my head throbs from drinking way too much wine last night, trying to numb the guilt of dodging my sister's fortieth-birthday celebration.

"You haven't heard from Celia today, have you?" he asks.

I pass through our messy living room, stopping to fold a blanket that has fallen off the La-Z-Boy currently containing my snoring husband.

"I haven't; why do you ask?" I grab the remote and mute the TV he left on all night, and then I collect the three empty beer bottles and walk them to the recycling bin in the kitchen.

"Woke up early this morning and she was gone. She left a note saying she'd be back, but it's almost ten . . ." His typical boisterous, uplifting voice is laced with a brand of timid uncertainty. "Tried calling her cell, but it goes straight to voice mail. I checked our security cameras, and she left around three thirty in the morning. I can't imagine where she'd be going that time of day . . ."

I tie up the overflowing trash and carry the stretched-out white bag to the garage.

"Maybe she went for a drive?" I ask.

"I thought so, too," he says. "I know she couldn't sleep last night, so I figured maybe she went out for some fresh air. Sometimes she does that . . . drives around listening to music when no one else is on the road. But if that's what she did, she'd be back by now."

I cradle the phone on my shoulder as I sort a stack of mail on the kitchen table, groaning when I get to an overdue water bill covered in yellow tape marked URGENT.

I gave Brad one job.

One.

It's not like we can't pay the bill—it's less than a hundred bucks. His truck payment is quintuple that and he never misses one of those.

"Yeah, that's really weird," I say to Rob—who I'm sure has never paid a bill late in his entire life because men like him have their priorities straight. "I can try reaching out to her?"

"It's no use if her phone's off, but feel free to try," he says. "Keep me posted if you hear anything, all right? I'll do the same."

I head to the hall bath to grab a shower so I can run to the grocery store and drop off the dry cleaning I asked my husband to take care of more than a week ago. Only I'm met with a locked door, the sound of water running, and my daughter Charlie's tinny pop music blaring from inside.

"Charlie? Five minutes, okay?" I knock on the door. "I need in."

"I just got in here," she yells back.

"That's fine, but finish up. I've got things to do." My daughter is notorious for her scorching thirty-minute showers that render us void of hot water for the hour that follows. "Charlie, did you hear me?"

"Yes!" she shouts back over some ear-bleeding song with questionable lyrics.

I make my way back to the living room to finish straightening up. It was never my intention to be the family maid, but I gave up years ago expecting these two to pick up after themselves. How anyone can live with clutter and chaos is beyond me, but Charlie and Brad are cut from the same cloth. It's as if they don't physically see the mess. They're blind to it. It's their superpower, I'm certain.

When I'm finished straightening pillows and placing random items back where they belong, I debate firing up the Hoover. As much pleasure as it would bring me to wake Brad from his gentle slumber, I'd rather enjoy a cup of coffee in peace.

So that's what I do.

And while my morning joe brews, I call my sister.

Just like Rob said, it goes straight to voice mail.

"Celia, it's Genevieve." I grab my favorite mug—a pink ceramic number that belonged to my mother before she passed—from the cupboard. "Um, Rob's looking for you, so I thought I'd try and reach out. He said you went for a drive or something in the middle of the night? I hope everything's okay. Please call me when you get this."

I debate tacking on a "hope you had a good birthday," but I opt against it.

It's too soon.

I end the call, pour my coffee, and take a seat at the kitchen table, waiting for my turn at the shower.

The window across from me offers a view into our quaint backyard—Celia and Rob's backyard if I'm being technical. They own the place. It was their starter home, which they claimed to have outgrown, though I'm not sure how two people can outgrow a home without expanding their family. Not a cat. Not a dog. Not even a goldfish. Yet somehow, they ran out of space.

For a while, I wondered if perhaps they were thinking of starting a family. Some people do that later in life. Or maybe they were thinking of fostering or adopting. I've yet to muster the nerve to ask her such a personal question. I have no idea where she stands with any of that.

Celia and I have been trying to mend our broken sisterhood for the bulk of my life. It wasn't until our mother passed away a couple of years ago that I reached out with the news and we found ourselves reconnecting.

It just so happened that at that point in time, Brad had lost his job, we'd fallen behind on the mortgage, and I'd just received the intent-to-foreclose notice from the bank. I didn't expect her to answer when I called. But she did. And in the hours that followed, I spilled my guts to a sister I barely knew . . . a sister I needed in my life more than I'd ever admitted . . . a sister I was too proud to admit I'd missed because I'd spent nearly two decades hating her, wishing she were dead—and carrying on as if she were.

She invited me to visit, even going so far as to take care of my plane ticket. And once I was there, she wasted no time offering to move us from Florida to Connecticut. In fact, their tenants had just moved out the week before and the house was sitting empty. She assured me Rob would be fine with it and that it would be nice getting to know me again. When I tried to bring up anything remotely related to our childhood or our parents, she'd cut me off with a gentle "that was then, this is now," or "the past is in the past." And when I asked if she had any interest in moving Celeste, too, she brushed it off with a "one thing at a time" response.

The guilt I'd felt for twenty years was gone . . . just like that. Whooshing like water under the bridge. While part of me was grateful to reconnect, the other part of me was furious. How many years did I spend in emotional anguish, mourning the relationship we didn't get a chance to have, only to have her wave it all away like it didn't matter?

And why couldn't she include Celeste, who had done nothing to deserve the abandonment she received?

"Charlie." I smack the bathroom door again. "It's been ten minutes. Time to get out."

A groan is followed by the squeak of the shower faucet shutting off.

"Is Charlie in there?" My husband stumbles down the hall, pointing at the locked bathroom door. His hair sticks up every which way as he scratches at his five-o'clock shadow. "I need to take a piss."

I take back my sentiments about Rob and Celia outgrowing this house. There's a reason modern-day primary bedrooms tend to have two sinks instead of one and the toilet gets its own room. There's nothing functional about this house. Three little bedrooms, one tiny bath, a kitchen with open upper shelves where cabinets should be.

The plan was to stay in this house until we got jobs and settled in; six months was the goal. Two years later, I'm working forty hours a week at a phone company call center and Brad is still unemployed.

The bathroom door swings open. Our teenage daughter steps out in a cloud of steam, her phone still blasting in her hand. She stops in her tracks, eyeing both of us as if we're the ones inconveniencing her, and then she squeezes past without a word.

Brad wastes no time helping himself to the bathroom, but to be fair, he had no idea I was next in line.

Charlie slams her bedroom door shut.

I slink against the wall, sliding down until I'm sitting in the hallway. Alone. Unneeded. Unwanted. Unappreciated.

I think back to Celia and myself as little girls, and how obsessed I was with her. From the time I took my first steps, I lived in her shadow. But the older we got, the more space she wanted. And by the time we hit our teenage years, the distance between us was canyon sized. That was also about the time she started getting in trouble. Asking questions. Disobeying. I learned early on to walk a straighter line than she ever could.

I didn't want to spend the night in the hell shack.

I didn't want to be told I was worthless, morally corrupt, or a black mark on the family name.

I didn't want to set a bad example for Celeste.

I didn't want to be sent away.

When Brad exits the bathroom, the toilet water is still draining. I'm willing to bet money we don't have that he didn't wash his hands. He never used to be like this . . . so sloppy and inconsiderate. In fact, when we first met, he was the preacher's son at our church—practically the most eligible bachelor in the entire congregation. My parents were over the moon when he asked my father if he could court me, and I felt honored that Pastor Jacobs's son chose me.

Honored.

The biggest running joke of my life.

Actually, no. The biggest running joke of my life would be that I did everything "right" and ended up married to a dejected shell of a man while raising a teenage daughter whose hatred of me goes beyond anything angst and hormones could explain.

Sprinkle in a bankruptcy, a constantly overdrawn checking account, and a DOA social life, and I'm one major life event away from becoming one of those women who demands to speak to the manager over the littlest of things.

I lock myself in the bathroom, twist the shower knob, and take a seat on the edge of the tub. Burying my head in my hands, I want to cry, but per usual, nothing comes out. Antidepressants have made it impossible for me to feel much of anything anymore.

Maybe it's for the best.

Peeling out of my clothes, I step under the spray of lukewarm water.

I let the droplets run down my cheeks in rivulets, the closest thing this face has felt to tears in a long time. And then I think of my sister. I wish I knew her well enough to know where she'd have gone, but the truth is, we're barely more than strangers—even after the move. All our exchanges have been superficial: small talk, recipe swaps, a quick mention of a new restaurant that opened in town. We're lucky if we make time for each other once or twice a month, though it beats not speaking at all.

I finish my shower, which is all but ice cold for the final two minutes, dry my hair, get dressed, grab my grocery list, and head to the store.

Halfway there, I check my phone at a red light just in case Celia called while I was busy.

But there's nothing.

Maybe it's a fruitless endeavor, but I call her again anyway.

Once again, it goes straight to voice mail.

Does she realize her husband is worried sick? Does she care? Or is she still the same old self-centered Celia she's always been, always looking out for number one?

Regardless, I leave a message because that's what good sisters do. I may not have a big, beautiful house, a happy marriage, or a closetful of pretty things, but it's not about what I have or don't have. It's about who I am.

And I am a good sister.

"Celia, it's me again . . ." I say. "Just making sure you're okay. Call me . . . please . . . bye."

CHAPTER 18

GENEVIEVE

Present day

I call Rob Saturday night, shortly before nine. "Any word from her yet?"

"Nothing." He exhales into the phone. In the background are what I can only assume are footsteps, and I imagine him pacing the polished marble floors of their sweeping manse. "I've called her every fifteen minutes. Left at least a dozen messages. Something's wrong, Genevieve. Celia would never leave in the middle of the night, and she certainly wouldn't shut off her phone."

"Have you contacted the police?"

"Of course I've contacted the police." His words have a bite to them, but I don't take it personally given the circumstances.

"What'd they say?"

"They had me file a report."

"And?"

"And they helped me track the OnStar on her SUV . . . found it at the Callahan train station."

"All right." I sit up in my bed and pause the TV show I was watching. "That's good, right? That means we have a general idea of where she went. Isn't that the route you guys usually take to New York? Maybe she went to the city?"

"Not necessarily . . . That station has service to every major city up and down the coast," he says. "I contacted our bank, though. Confirmed there was a transaction at five twenty-two this morning. The police are trying to work with the train station to narrow down the transaction and see what kind of ticket she bought, but these things take time."

"All right. So we know she couldn't sleep last night," I say, assembling the facts out loud. "She got up. Left you a note saying she'd be back. She went for a drive. Somehow ended up at the Callahan train station and bought a ticket to . . . somewhere."

"Yeah," he sighs.

"Did she take anything with her?"

"Not that I can tell. Everything's here except her purse and her phone."

I fling the covers off my legs and climb out of bed. "Did they ping her phone?"

"They can't when it's off." His voice is monotone, as if he's given this information a million times already today.

"So what are they doing to find her?" I ask.

"They're doing what they can, but she's considered 'not at risk' because she left a note," he says. "She's considered a 'voluntarily absent spouse' or some shit like that."

I mean, I understand. There are laws in place to protect spouses who need to flee abusive relationships, and the police have no way of knowing if that's the case here.

I peek out my window, into my admittedly cozy neighborhood with its admittedly nice neighbors who mostly keep to themselves. The houses are filled with warm evening light, flickering TVs, and faceless folks carrying on with their lives.

"I can't, for the life of me, figure out why she'd get on a train somewhere and turn off her phone," Rob says. His voice breaks over the last few words. "It doesn't make sense, Gen. It's not her."

He's never called me "Gen" before.

I guess now that he needs a shoulder to cry on, we're comrades?

I've never been crazy about the guy . . . something to do with a thirty-one-year-old grown man running off with my eighteen-year-old, sheltered, virginal sister. It never sat right with me. Even at sixteen, I knew it was dubious. As the years ticked by and Celia never came home, we all assumed the worst despite Rob's parents being stout members of our church community. He cut off all communication with them just like Celia cut off all communication with us. At least that's what Rob's parents told us. We never had a reason to believe they were lying.

Though now, at thirty-eight years of age, I've been around long enough to know that people lie all the time. Good people, too. There isn't a person on God's green earth who hasn't told a fib at some point.

We all have our reasons.

Perhaps Rob's parents were trying to protect Celia? Not that I'd know. She and I have never discussed that phase in our lives—one I always referred to as "the great divide" because it delineated the first part of my life from everything that took place after she left. My sister prefers to act as though it never happened.

I couldn't pretend if I tried.

Her departure from our family was profound in ways she'll never comprehend because the past is a subject she won't touch with a ten-foot pole.

"Rob," I say. "Celia is a runner. When things get overwhelming for her, she runs. When we were younger, anytime things would get to be too much, she'd . . . disappear for a little while. Sometimes she'd hide in a kitchen cabinet. Other times a closet. Once she climbed a tree and sat up there for hours. My mother was beside herself trying to find her, and all she had to do was look up. Is there anything you can think of that would've upset her over the past twenty-four hours? Anything at all?"

"I've racked my brain all day . . . and I can't come up with a damn thing," he says. "She seemed to be enjoying herself at the party, and when we got home, we carried in all the gifts and cards and headed up to bed. She couldn't sleep. She got up. That was it." Rob pauses for a moment before dragging in a haggard breath on the other end of the line. "You know, she opened all of her birthday gifts before she left. I came down and found everything neatly organized on the dining room table, like she had it all set up so she could come back and write thank-you cards."

"Did someone give her something that would've upset her?" It's a ridiculous question given that she was surrounded by people who clearly think she hung the moon (or at least act like it), but I have to ask.

"Not that I could tell? I saw a vase. A robe. Gift cards. A bracelet. Nothing out of the ordinary?"

"Maybe . . . maybe it's an age thing? Some women feel a certain way when they hit forty. Like they've hit this milestone where they've reached the back end of their life and their youth is forever gone. A point of no return."

The year Celia left home for good was also the year my mother turned forty. It was like a switch had been flipped. She prayed for hours every day, read books about Heaven and angels, and became obsessed with Judgment Day. I always thought it was because she'd reached middle age, though in retrospect it's likelier that she was worried she'd be sent to hell for raising a wayward daughter.

"That's ridiculous," Rob says. "Celia isn't like that. Age and vanity are the least of her concerns."

I don't know if they're the least of her concerns, per se. I've seen what her hairstylist charges. And she's admitted to things like "baby Botox," diamond facials, and "dabbling with" filler. Her clothes aren't cheap by any means: $100 leggings for lounging, $200 cross-trainers, limited-edition bags, designer straps for her Apple Watch so they can coordinate with any and all looks. I wouldn't say she's vain, but she certainly takes pride in maintaining herself. That or she's filling some kind of void, though I'm not sure what. From the outside looking in, my sister lives the fullest of lives.

That said, with all the pressure society places on women to not age, I can see how a fortieth birthday could send someone into an emotional tailspin if the conditions are right. And seeing how I'm still getting to know my sister, I don't think my theory is complete rubbish.

Still, Rob misunderstood me.

"I don't mean youth as it pertains to beauty or looks." I clear my throat. "I mean, youth as in . . . you know, being that much closer to death."

"What do you mean?"

"When we were kids, Celia had this thing about death. She was terrified of dying because she was scared of what comes next," I say. "Maybe it was all those years of my parents preaching fire and brimstone at us, but it was the not knowing that would get to her. She couldn't walk past a cemetery or go to a funeral without having a full-on panic attack."

Rob is quiet for a beat.

"She isn't a fan of attending funerals, I know that," he says. "She'll always send flowers in lieu of . . . says she can't bear to see someone who was once alive . . . in a lifeless state. I figured we all have our hang-ups and that was hers. Some people are afraid of spiders or the dark. Celia was afraid of seeing dead people."

"So maybe she's freaking out because she's officially reached middle age and feels like she's that much closer to dying?"

He groans. "It's far-fetched, Genevieve. Your idea. I know my wife. She wouldn't get upset about her age and then . . . disappear into the city with her phone off. It doesn't make sense."

"You're right. None of this makes sense." I feel as if someone ripped an important document into a million tiny shreds and I'm trying to fit them together in some sensical sort of way. "She'll turn up. She always did before. Celia never stayed gone for very long."

Except after she ran off with Rob . . .

For years, I hoped she'd show up at the door one day, throw her arms around us, and tell us what a mistake she'd made. I secretly yearned for Rob to break her heart so she'd be taught a lesson. I wanted her back. I *needed* her back.

It was exhausting being the oldest child in the house, having the burden of perfection placed on me so as not to corrupt our innocent Celeste.

I wasn't half as brave or resourceful as Celia was. I fantasized about leaving, but my fantasies always involved getting caught because that's exactly what would've happened. So I stayed. I chose the easier option, the option that felt safest at the time. And while I was at home, living the life I was told to live, Celia was out there somewhere, living the life she always wanted.

Jealousy all but ate through me some nights.

"She's a grown woman," I continue. "Not some teenager running away from home to prove a point to her parents. You two have a happy marriage." As far as I know. "She has no reason to abandon you."

Heavy silence settles between us. Perhaps "abandon" was too strong of a word to use, but it's one I've always associated with her. It rolled off my tongue before I could catch it.

"What the hell do I do now?" His voice is broken when he speaks again.

I bite the inside of my lip, not knowing what to say. My father never showed emotion, and the one and only instance my husband has shed a tear was the first time he held Charlie in his arms.

I don't know how to comfort broken or emotional men. I don't know how to comfort anyone, really. It's difficult to do something I was never taught or shown. It's unnatural, like speaking a foreign language for the first time.

"What can I do to help?" I ask. Maybe I can't lend him a shoulder to cry on, but I'm good at getting things done, at making things happen.

"I wish there *was* something you could do. They told me just to stay home, wait by my phone in case she calls—or in case they call with an update."

"So are they actively looking for her?"

"No," he says. "Aside from working with the train station to isolate her ticket, they've done everything they can do for now. Unless I can prove she's in immediate danger, they're not going to send out a search party or plaster her face on the news."

"Have you reached out to any of her friends? Maybe someone knows something? Or maybe she's been in touch with one of them?"

"I called a few of them, yes. No one has heard anything."

I slump back into my bed and bury my forehead against my palm. "Okay, well, let's hope for the best for now. And first thing in the morning, I'm coming over and we're putting together a game plan—assuming she doesn't come home tonight."

"You don't have to do—"

"Rob," I interrupt him. "When we were kids and she'd disappear, I was the one who always found her. And it was the strangest thing . . . I'd have a gut feeling, an instinct. I could just sense her presence, if that makes sense. If they're not going to look for her, then I will."

I don't know how I could possibly find her now—in a state that still feels like a strange, foreign land to me most days. But I'd like to think that I could. Maybe then she'd see me for who I really am: a loyal sister who only ever wanted to be close to her, to feel like a part of her world.

"I'll keep you posted if she shows up," Rob says. Any hint of hope or optimism in his voice is gone.

"If I don't hear from you, I'll be at your door first thing in the morning." I end the call as my husband stumbles into our room, his eyes red and bleary as if he fell asleep watching TV and then woke up and decided to sleep in an actual bed tonight instead of his favorite recliner.

"Any sign of her yet?" he asks.

I sit up, taken aback that he actually remembered what I told him earlier today. He was watching ESPN when I said Celia was missing, and he gave me zero indication that he was listening to a word I said. He kept saying, "Mm-hmm . . . wow . . . that's crazy . . ."

"No," I say. "Nothing."

He peels the covers off his side of the bed and climbs in beside me. "So . . . is anyone looking for her or what?"

"Rob filed a police report. All they know is she bought a train ticket at five twenty-two this morning."

"Weird." He reaches for his lamp, turning out the light. His half of the room grows gray and dark. "I'm sure she'll turn up."

"I'm going over there first thing in the morning," I say. "So you'll have to take Charlie to her babysitting job at ten o'clock . . . the Hinkleys on Tenth Street. And pick her up at one if I'm not back by then. Also, make sure her phone is charged. She forgets to do that sometimes."

"Yep," he says, rolling to his side.

Heaven help me if I were to ever go missing. I don't think Brad could muster up the energy to drive himself to the police station to file a report.

I turn out my light and lie next to my husband, listening to him sawing logs in his sleep while I stare at the ceiling. As much as I've disliked Rob over the years, as much as I wanted so badly for him to be the biggest mistake my sister ever made . . . I can't deny he cares about her—which is more than I can say for Brad.

They say fortune favors the bold, and it must be true, because Celia was always the boldest sister. After everything she's been through, she always lands on her feet and walks away with better circumstances than she had before.

Whatever made her leave . . .

Wherever she went . . .

Whenever she comes home . . .

She's going to be fine.

I refuse to believe this time will be different from any other.

CHAPTER 19

GENEVIEVE

Present day

Rob sits hunched over in his favorite living room chair Sunday morning, his elbows on his bouncing knees and his fingers forming a steeple. I was hoping I wouldn't have to come here today—hoping Celia would show up sometime in the middle of the night with a perfectly logical explanation.

But that call never came.

So here I am.

Our phones are resting side by side on the coffee table, next to two untouched mugs of coffee. I tried calling her again on my way here, hoping in vain that it wouldn't go to voice mail again.

"I've gone through every scenario," he says. His knees stop bouncing, but only for a second. "I can't think of a single thing that would've led to her leaving like this."

"Why aren't the police taking this more seriously? I mean, she's been missing twenty-four hours now, isn't there some kind of—"

"The twenty-four-hour thing is a myth," he says. "Urgency is based on whether or not the person is believed to be in danger. With the note and her leaving of her own accord, they have no reason to suspect . . ."

He can't finish his thought, but he doesn't need to. Neither one of us wants to say the words "something happened to her."

"So you're just supposed to sit around and wait?" I ask.

He grimaces before burying his face in his hands. "Yeah. Pretty much."

"Did they at least assign someone to the case?"

Rob nods. "Yep. Some detective named Sean Samuels. He seems to know what he's doing, but I get the sense he's spread paper thin. He's been helpful at least, and he asks all the right questions. Questions I wouldn't think to ask, checking things I wouldn't think to check. But he can't make her reappear out of thin air. For now, they're sending her photo to every precinct in the area."

Rob's tone is more hopeless than hopeful.

Deflated, I lean back against the sofa, resting my elbow on its leather arm and staring at the marble-inlayed fireplace across the room. The mantel is lined with at least a dozen photos of the two of them on various excursions. I home in on the biggest one. The two of them grinning, tanned, taut, and tropical drinks in hand as the sun sets over the ocean behind them. The image beside them, in a gold foil frame, shows the happy couple perched on the edge of a boat, wearing yellow rain slickers, a beautiful waterfall in the background. But it's the third picture that catches my attention: an image of a much younger Rob and Celia. He's in khakis and a white button-down, she's in a floral dress, and a man in a black judge's robe stands between them. It must be their wedding photo.

While I've always envied the fact that my sister found her Prince Charming and built the kind of life that gave our childhood the middle finger, I've always wondered if she was truly happy with him . . . or if she was simply trading one hell for another.

The pictures on the fireplace mantel seem to answer the question. They show me that my sister was content, in love, and living her dream.

But if her life was so great . . . why'd she run away?

The house is too quiet, the lack of Celia's presence acting like an invisible void. It always seems like anytime someone goes missing, there's more fanfare. Newspeople banging on the door. Reporters blowing up phones begging for a statement. Police camped outside the house. But maybe that's only on TV. Hundreds of thousands of people disappear every year—at least that's what my Google search told me this morning. Celia is a drop of water in a vast ocean of missing people.

I pull out my phone and open the Notes app. "Can you tell me who all was at the party Friday night?" I ask. "I want to make a list."

He wrinkles his nose. "Why?"

"I thought I'd start talking to people, see if they know anything . . ."

"I gave all of that information to the detective already."

"Is there something wrong with doubling down?" I lift a brow, my fingers hovering over my phone, waiting.

"I already reached out to most of them yesterday when I was trying to find her." His mouth twists at the side. "They were just as baffled as I am. I don't want to harass people who had nothing to do with this . . . her friends, our friends . . . they're good people. They're already worried sick. Detective Samuels will reach out to them soon . . ."

"With all due respect, Rob, what my sister did was bizarre. And maybe you've been married to her for the last twenty-odd years and you think you know what she would and wouldn't do, but you say she was fine Friday night. Clearly she wasn't. Clearly something happened to make her leave. All I'm saying is, maybe you don't know her as well as you thought you did. And maybe it wouldn't hurt for me to talk to her friends?"

He sinks into his chair, letting his hands fall limp in his lap.

"*With all due respect*, Genevieve," he says, echoing my earlier statement, "she lives a pretty charmed life."

I resist the urge to roll my eyes. His wife is missing and all he can say is she lives a charmed life? Is he implying that women with enviable lives are incapable of being unhappy?

"Something had to have upset her is all I'm getting at," I say. "Something set her off."

He pinches the bridge of his aquiline nose, his lips moving, but nothing comes out. "Maybe . . ."

He pauses.

"Maybe what?" I lean forward.

"I got a job offer a few weeks back—from a hospital in Kansas City," he says. "I haven't officially accepted it. Maybe . . . maybe she's upset about the possibility of moving? Maybe seeing all her friends at the party made her think about what we'd be leaving behind?" He sits straighter, his palms flattening against the air. "But if she was upset about that, she never said a word to me. In fact, when I told her the news, I expected to have some pushback, but she smiled, like she was happy about it. And she never really brought it up again after that. Maybe she needed more time to digest it. Maybe it didn't feel real until Friday night."

I don't ask if Rob counts *me* among her friends.

There's a tightness in my chest when I think of Celia being more upset about leaving her friends behind than her own sister. Maybe we weren't close, but we were getting there.

We were trying.

Baby steps.

"Not once did she ask me not to accept the job, and believe me, if she'd expressed an ounce of doubt, I'd have said no," Rob continues. "I know it's asking a lot to have her uproot her entire world. And of course, I expected her to feel guilty about your whole situation."

I sniff. "My . . . whole . . . situation? What's that mean?"

"You know, she moved you and your family up here so the two of you could reconnect," he says. "I think she feels responsible for you for whatever reason. Like she needs to take care of you, be the big sister she never was."

I roll my eyes. "I didn't ask her to do any of that."

"But you didn't say no."

"Her offer was generous, and it came at a point in my life when saying no wasn't exactly an option. It was either move here or be homeless. What would you have chosen?"

His jaw sets as our eyes lock. While everyone else sees Rob as a friendly everyman with boy-next-door charm, I've always reserved my judgment. There's a curious glint in his eye whenever he's around me. I don't think Celia's ever noticed—or if she has, she's never addressed it. But a person can tell when someone else is smiling at them yet thinking thoughts that don't match the expression on their face. It's always in their eyes, that hint of something else. Something darker.

I have no way of knowing what all Celia has told him about me over the years. When Celia came back from that reformatory, she was cold and distant to me, making no bones about the fact that she considered me a rat and a traitor. She blamed me for her getting sent away, but I was just a kid. I thought I was doing the right thing, and I was genuinely worried for her soul at the time. My parents filled my head with all kinds of terrifying tales of fiery infernos and damned souls. If I'd let Celia leave that first time and my parents found out I knew where she was and didn't tell them, I'd have suffered a fate much worse than anything they could've inflicted on her.

Celia lived in torture.

But I lived in fear.

"I'm sorry." Rob rises from his chair. "I shouldn't get short with you, and I don't mean to rub any of this in your face. I know you're just trying to help."

He strides into the next room, returning with a sheet of paper, which he hands to me before sitting down once again.

"This is a copy of the list I gave to the police. It's everyone who was at the party, their addresses, and their phone numbers. Plus one person who wasn't there."

"Who was that?" I scan the scribbled numbers and letters.

"Isabel Delvy," he says. "She was one of Celia's closest friends, but the two of them had a falling-out a couple of months ago."

I remember Isabel. Celia introduced us shortly after I moved here, taking us both out to brunch at some highbrow spot that I was embarrassingly underdressed for. Isabel spent the entirety of the time discussing inside jokes and doing everything she could to make me feel like a third wheel. Or at least that's what it felt like. She even scooched her chair a little closer to Celia's, like she was picking sides. And every time Celia said something cute or funny, Isabel would laugh the loudest or put her hand over Celia's and praise her for being *witty* or *hilarious* or whatever adjective happened to tumble out of her bee-stung lips in that moment.

If my sister had a fan club, Isabel would be the president.

"What happened?" I ask.

"Not completely sure, to tell you the truth," Rob says. "Celia said it was over something trite, that she'd give me the details another time. She said Isabel would come around eventually, so she didn't want to waste time dwelling on it. A couple of times, I attempted to bring it up to her, only she'd swat her hand and say it wasn't worth talking about. But I always saw the hurt in her eyes when I'd say Isabel's name. Whatever happened, it cut her deep. Those two were inseparable and then they just stopped talking. It couldn't have been easy for her."

Celia never mentioned anything about Isabel to me, but then again our conversations were always superficial in nature.

"I tried to extend an olive branch by inviting her to the birthday party," Rob says. "But she never replied to the invite, and she never showed up."

I think of Isabel and her chiseled yet feminine jawline, her pillowy lips, and her deep-set aquamarine eyes. She was tall, nothing but legs and sharp angles, but there was a softness to her as well, in the way that she moved—at least when it pertained to my sister. But it went both ways. Celia seemed a little more at ease whenever Isabel was beside her, like she could let her guard down and not be so perfect and put together, like she could say anything she wanted without being judged.

I'll admit, I felt the sting of jealousy anytime I saw the two of them together around town—which was often. It wasn't unusual to spot them having coffee at La Diem almost every morning after their Bikram yoga class or catch them dashing out of the nail salon, beaming as they walked in lockstep to their cars.

Rob wasn't exaggerating when he said they were inseparable.

The bond they shared rivaled the kind of sisterhood I always wanted to have with Celia.

The sisterhood we should have had.

The sisterhood we *would* have had, had Celia never left.

CHAPTER 20

Genevieve

Present day

"Dad?" My phone is hot against my palm Sunday afternoon. "It's Gen."

We haven't spoken since I left Cross Beach two years ago. After Mom passed, he wasted no time marrying a widowed church member at the new pastor's suggestion. It was a "match made in heaven," the new pastor said at the time, going so far as to claim that my mother came to him in a dream and said she wanted them to be together.

He clears his throat, breathing into the phone. I imagine him in his Sunday best, having just returned home after an hours-long sermon.

"I know who it is. I have caller ID," he says. There's no elation in his tone. He isn't pleased to be hearing from me, not that he should be. In his eyes, I chose Celia over him when I left our hometown two years ago.

"Do you have a second?" I ask.

"Esta was just about to make lunch," he says as if I'm inconveniencing him. But my skin is thicker now than it once was. "I have a minute. What's going on?"

"It's about Celia." I hold my breath for a beat. "She's missing and we can't find her. We're worried something happened . . ."

"And what do you propose *I* do about this?" He chuckles, like this is amusing to him. "That girl is dead to me, Genevieve. She's been dead to me for twenty years."

I wasn't expecting sympathy or support; I simply wanted to let him know. Despite their estrangement, he's still her father. If, God forbid, Charlie and I ever had a falling-out in her adulthood and something happened to her, I'd want to know immediately.

"Celia has always been good at getting herself into trouble," he says. "If she's not dead yet, she's better off that way. She was too weak for this world. Never could talk an ounce of sense into that thick skull of hers. She walked around like she knew better than all of us." He sniffs, speaking of her with zero emotion, like a breeder discarding the weakest littermate.

"All right, well, I just wanted you to know," I say.

"Thank you for thinking of me, Genevieve, as I'm sure I'm not always on your mind, but this wasn't necessary."

He doesn't segue the conversation, doesn't ask how I'm doing or inquire about Brad or Charlie. He doesn't so much as offer to pray for any of us.

Celia, my mother, me . . . we all abandoned him.

We're all dead to him now, buried in the ground or not.

"I'm going to eat my lunch now. Esta's waiting for me. You should call your sister when you get a chance—Celeste, that is," he says before ending the call without so much as a goodbye.

I have half a mind to delete his number, to write him off once and for all the way he writes everyone else off, but instead I gather a deep breath and focus on the task at hand.

I'll call Celeste later, not that she'll likely care. Over the years, my parents treated Celia's absence like she was a daughter who died tragically young. Eventually her photographs were put away and her name stopped being spoken. Celeste was too young to remember her, too young to miss her. I doubt she thinks of her often these days, if at all.

I scan the list of names and addresses Rob gave me before heading to Charlie's room. The door is propped open, and she's lying on her stomach at the foot of her bed, paging through a glossy magazine, white earbuds popped in.

"Charlie," I say. She doesn't hear me. *"Charlie."*

She taps her phone screen, pausing her music, and then removes a single bud. "What?"

"I need to take off for a couple of hours. Just wanted to tell you. Call me if you need anything," I say.

"Are you going to the store? Because I need more face wash. The foaming one in the blue bottle."

She doesn't ask about her missing aunt; nor does she inquire about how I'm doing or if there's any way she can help. This is Charlie's world; we just live in it.

"Tell your dad I'll be home around dinnertime," I say before leaving.

As much as I'd like to be upset with her shortsighted self-centeredness, she's the product of her environment. Brad and I have raised her to be the center of our world, so why would she worry about anything beyond her own personal orbit? For years, we tried having another child, running up all our credit cards with fruitless IUI cycles and taking out a personal loan to pay for a (failed) round of IVF. Sometimes I wonder if Charlie would be a little less *Charlie* had we given her a brother or sister. Other times I'm doubtful. She hasn't grown up with aunts, uncles, cousins, or grandparents in the traditional sense—save for Brad's parents. For the most part, it's always been the three of us, and Charlie has always been priority one. She's the glue keeping our loveless marriage together. Or maybe that's what I tell myself to feel better about staying with a man who stopped looking at me and started looking through me years ago.

I head out to the driveway to leave a moment later, stopping when I find Brad waxing his midnight-blue Ram. A country song plays from the interior speakers as he buffs the driver's-side door.

"I'm taking off for a bit," I tell him.

"They find Celia?" he asks without looking up.

"No," I say. "Not yet. Thought I'd go talk to some of her friends."

"Sure you should get involved like that?" He snaps his neon-green spearmint gum, his hands resting on the small of his back as he stretches. His shirt is oil stained and faded. He hasn't shaved in almost a week. At some point in our marriage, he stopped caring, and I stopped noticing that he stopped caring, and now here we are.

"Someone has to. The police aren't doing much because they don't think she's in immediate danger, but it's been almost a day and a half now and her phone is still off." I throw my hands in the air. There's no point in explaining any of this to Brad because either he won't care or he won't remember. "Anyway. I'll be back later."

I climb inside my car and plug the first address into my phone's GPS.

Ten minutes later, I pull up in front of an ostentatious white Colonial, one with two cast-iron jockeys at the end of the driveway holding lanterns—the ones certain affluent New Englanders have adopted without realizing their racist origins.

Ignorance is bliss, I suppose.

I park behind a glistening white Porsche Panamera and head to the front door, ringing the bell and standing back. A moment later, a man with a face much younger than his snow-white hair would suggest answers.

"Hi, are you Neal?" I ask. "I'm Genevieve, Celia Guest's sister."

His eyes are expressive and round. "Oh, my goodness. Yes. Has she come home yet?"

"No," I say. "We're still looking for her. I was hoping you and your wife might have a moment to talk? I just have a few questions."

His brows knit in the middle. "Deanna's just getting up from a nap, but sure, come on in."

"I don't want to impose . . ."

He motions for me to follow him in. "No imposition at all. Deanna's been undergoing chemotherapy, so she hasn't been feeling the best lately. She's quite upset about the situation with Celia, so I know she'd be happy to help any way that she can. If you want to have a seat in the living room, I'll go grab her and we'll be down shortly."

I take a seat in a room filled with furniture arranged in a way that's more conducive to conversation than watching television. In fact, there isn't a TV in sight. Just a framed oil painting hanging over the fireplace and a collection of potted plants, designer pillows, and pricey-looking vases, urns, crystal jars, coffee table books, and glass beads placed just so.

"Genevieve?" A thin woman in a silk Pucci head wrap and kelly-green dress shuffles my way, a matching tweed jacket cinched around her narrow waist and thick blue-framed glasses covering her pale face. I remember Celia mentioning that one of her good friends has been sick lately, but I never caught the name. The lady standing before me looks every bit the part of someone going through *something*. "I'm Deanna. My husband said you wanted to talk to me about Celia?"

Deanna places a hand over her heart, her lips turning down at the sides.

"Rob called me yesterday asking if I'd heard from her," Deanna says, getting right to it. "And then he told me he couldn't get a hold of her. I'm just completely beside myself, worried sick." She takes a spot on the couch across from me, her slight frame barely putting a dent in the stiff pillows. "Is there anything we can do to help?"

"So." I clear my throat. "As you know, Celia and I were estranged for quite some time. Because of that, I'm afraid I don't know her as well as some of her inner-circle friends. I just wanted to ask a few questions. I know there's a detective working on the case, so I apologize if any of these are redundant. I'm just trying to piece things together on my own."

Her lips press together and she nods. "Ask anything you need."

"In your opinion, was Celia herself at the party Friday night?" I brace, praying she doesn't ask why I wasn't there.

Deanna's lips pull into a kind yet bittersweet smile. "She was every bit herself. And then some. She was radiant, glowing. It's been a long time since I've seen her that happy."

"Long time . . . Are you saying she wasn't happy before?"

Her espresso-dark eyes turn round. "Oh, I wasn't implying that at all. I just mean, she was on cloud nine, mood-wise. I mean, wouldn't you be? Your husband throws you a lavish birthday party and all of your favorite people are there."

Imagining my sister among all her favorite people—myself excluded—stings. But I brush it off.

Deanna clasps her fragile hands together and leans forward, chin tucked. "Celia's friends are everything to her, as I'm sure you know. Her friends are . . . well, they're like family to her. They *are* her family."

Another burn, though she doesn't seem like the kind of person to make intentional jabs, and I doubt my sister has shared her messy past with her societal friends.

I swallow the knot in my throat.

"Of course," I say. "Aside from Friday night, is there anything you can think of that she might have been struggling with? Anything at all? Marital issues, perhaps?"

She lifts her brows, lips pressed into a thin line.

"I don't mean to be so blunt. I also don't mean to put you on the spot," I say. "Rob says everything between them was wonderful. I assume he told the police the same thing . . . I have no way of knowing if that's true or not."

Without warning, her husband crosses the threshold from the dining room into the living room, a glass of water and a medication bottle in hand.

"Sorry to interrupt," he says. "Deanna, it's time for your next dose."

"One moment, please, Genevieve." Deanna swallows a handful of various-colored pills with delicate sips of water. "Thank you, sweetheart." He leaves us be, and she straightens her shoulders, eyes pointed at the crystal candy jar on the coffee table between us. "I'm not sure if you're aware, but I was diagnosed with late-stage lymphoma earlier this year. Treatment has been . . . challenging . . . exhausting . . ." She glances toward the doorway where her husband came and went. "Neal has been an absolute godsend, by my side every step of the way. And your sister, when she first got news of my diagnosis, she was the first to show up at my door offering a shoulder to cry on."

Tears threaten to disturb my vision, but I blink them away. The thought of my sister showing such compassion and selflessness, when it was never taught to us, makes me happy for her.

"She also organized a meal train for us," Deanna says. "The treatment was completely obliterating my appetite, and cooking even the most basic meal was exhausting, so she took it upon herself to make sure I didn't have to worry about feeding my family. Neal and the kids had the most delicious lunches and dinners every single day that first month. And each week, she'd drop off a basket of Popsicles and ginger tea and shea-butter lotions for me. No one asked her to do any of that; she just wanted to help." Deanna peers down at her folded hands. "She's always doing so much for everyone else. It pains me not being able to help. I wish I had some sort of information to share, something that would unlock a secret. But Celia was one of the happiest people I knew. Oh, goodness." She covers her face with her hand, her postage stamp–sized diamond glimmering in the afternoon sun. "I don't mean to speak of her in past tense."

I didn't realize.

"I can't tell you what I don't know. But I can tell you what I do know, and it's that Celia and Rob have a beautiful relationship," she says. "I've never seen either of them raise their voice at one another. Anytime we were with them, they'd always give each other that look.

You know, the look. Like they were still young and in love and not some middle-aged couple who'd been together for decades. They travel all the time. They're involved in the community. They have their hobbies and interests—shared and separate. For instance, he prefers racquetball, while she prefers to swim. They love film, though, and they never miss the local festival that the college puts on. Little things like that. All in all, they're a very pleasant couple, and we always look forward to our dinner dates with them."

"Okay, well," I say, worrying the inside of my lip, "I appreciate all of that, Deanna. If anything comes up, please don't hesitate to reach out to me. I got your number from Rob, so I'll text you—that way you have mine."

She pushes herself up from the couch and escorts me to the front door with small, careful steps.

"Celia and Rob have standing dinner reservations with Holly and Peter Lancaster every week," she tells me as I leave. "You might ask them if anything seemed amiss lately? Everyone in this town talks. If there's trouble in paradise, Holly's usually the first to know . . ."

"Thank you," I say.

I call Holly once inside my car. She invites me over before I finish my spiel. True gossip queens can smell good dirt from miles away. I imagine she's hoping to glean some inside information from me. Unfortunately for her, it's likely to be the other way around—assuming she knows anything.

I won't hold my breath.

I have a feeling no one knows the true side of Celia, the side she kept only for herself.

CHAPTER 21

GENEVIEVE

Present day

"Genevieve, come on in." Holly opens the door to her brick McMansion the second my foot hits the second step of her front stoop. "How are you doing? How are you holding up?"

She places her arm around me, her ice-blonde, beach-waved extensions bouncing over her shoulders as she leads me to her kitchen. An all-white-everything kind of kitchen, a room so immaculate it's either recently renovated or never used.

"Here, have a seat." She pulls a chair out from her table and then takes the spot beside me. A white gardenia candle flickers in the centerpiece, the wax hardly melted at all, like she lit it mere minutes ago. This is a woman who cares what people think—which means she cares what people say, too. I'm hopeful she'll have useful information for me. "Rob called me yesterday, and I've just been . . . well, it's all I can think about. Where is she? It's so strange, the whole thing."

"Yeah, we're all very confused by this," I say, "which is why I wanted to talk to you."

Her left brow arches, as if she doesn't comprehend the reason for my visit—and why would she? She talked over me during our phone call from the second I identified myself.

"Okay?" she asks.

"So Rob says he can't think of anything that would've upset Celia Friday night," I say. "He mentioned a couple of things that might have upset her in the last month or two, but I wanted to get your take. I was over at Deanna's a little while ago and she mentioned that if anything was going on, you might know about it."

Holly half chuckles, rolling her eyes. "Typical Deanna and her passive-aggressive remarks."

I jut my chin forward. "I don't think she meant to be offensive; she just gave me the impression that you—"

"I talk to everyone, about everything, yeah, I know. I've heard it before. I'm terrible at keeping secrets . . . and I tell everyone that up front. All of my new friends, they get the heads-up. They get a crash course in Holly 101. Same goes for you, Genevieve. I can't promise that anything you tell me today won't be repeated." She shrugs as if to apologize and yet not apologize at the same time. "I like to talk. I'm a bit of a social butterfly. Just being honest."

"I appreciate that." I gather in a lungful of her gardenia candle–scented air.

"How's Rob doing? Is he hanging in there? I keep thinking about calling him, but I don't want to be a pest. I'm sure he's just beside himself."

"He's not doing so great," I say. "I was over there this morning. I could tell he hasn't slept—understandably."

"What are the police saying?" she asks, and I remind myself anything I tell her will spread like wildfire through the community. God forbid someone in her inner circle has anything to do with this—I'd hate to tip them off.

"Not much of anything so far." I leave it at that.

"Really?" Her expression sours. "Are they even looking for her or what?"

"She's considered a not-at-risk absent spouse or something like that," I say. I'm probably butchering the technical term, but that's beside the point. "They're looking into different things, but so far they're just as puzzled as we are."

"Ugh." She clucks her tongue. "That's unacceptable. Celia Guest is . . . That woman is the backbone of Schofield. Everyone knows her. Everyone loves her. I keep watching the news thinking they're going to mention her, and they never do. If this community knew she was missing, she'd have an army of thousands looking for her."

"That would be amazing—if we knew where to look . . ."

Holly slices her hand through the air. "This is all Greek to me. I don't know the first thing about law enforcement protocol or how any of this is handled. I can't even stomach an episode of *Dateline* because it gets me so anxious, I want to throw up. And then I get nightmares and all of that. This is just . . . The mind can go down a very deep, dark alley with this stuff, and I'm trying to stay positive. I just . . . It's all so peculiar."

"Exactly," I say. "Is there anything—anything at all—that you can think of that she might have been upset about? When we were kids, Celia used to run off and hide when things were overwhelming. She'd disappear for a few hours, but she'd always come back. Can you think of something that might have triggered her after the birthday party? Or something that'd been bothering her lately?"

Holly picks at one of her fingernails before smoothing her palms over her snug leopard-print lululemon leggings.

"I don't want to compromise the investigation with hearsay," she says.

My heart dials up a notch, and my attention goes into overdrive.

"People talk all the time and . . ." Her words fade into nothing. "It's just . . . I spoke to Monique Denman this morning. She's a mutual friend of ours. And Monique said that when she was working on renovating Celia's primary bath last year, she was doing some organizing and found an entire basket filled with pill bottles. They were mostly for sleep and anxiety. And I get it. No judgment. We all need to take the edge off sometimes. But it was just something that really stood out to Monique—and to me, too—because you look at someone like Celia, who has it all, who does everything with a smile on her face, who makes you feel like you've known her your entire life, who seems to let life ricochet off of her so easily, and then you realize . . . she's only human." Holly gathers in a long breath and lets it go. *"She's just like us."*

My sister taking pills for her anxiety isn't exactly the bombshell this case needs to be blown wide open, but at least it gives me insight. If anything, it's confirmation that no matter how far my sister has come, she has things that keep her up at night like anyone else.

I'd be lying if I said I didn't take comfort in knowing that her life wasn't all peaches and cream after she left Cross Beach. Maybe she and Rob aren't as perfect as they seem? Maybe deep down she's just as miserable as everyone else?

"Okay, that's good to know," I say. "Anything else you can think of?"

Holly squints. "Nothing I can say definitively."

I pause. I read in a magazine article once that when you're interviewing someone, you should do your best to remain as quiet as possible. Let them do all the talking and eventually they'll tell you everything you want to know.

"So I've been friends with Celia for seven . . . maybe eight years now? And I've never known her to celebrate her birthday," she says. "Now this is pure speculation on my part. One of those things that just don't add up. Granted, I know it was her fortieth birthday, so it was a milestone or whatever. But in years past, Celia flat out refused to so much as acknowledge her birthday. It kind of became a running joke. Every year when June fourteenth would roll around, I'd send her a text like . . . 'a little birdie told me it's time to renew your driver's license.' Things that implied I was aware that it was her birthday but I wasn't actually celebrating it. She always seemed to get a kick out of it—or she was good at pretending she did anyway."

I nod. "We weren't allowed to celebrate our birthdays as kids."

She lifts a brow while splaying a hand over her heart. "Really? I had no idea. That's so sad."

Holly's ignorance only serves to confirm what I suspected—Celia likely never spoke about her past to her friends.

"But what I'm getting at here," Holly continues, "is that Rob taking the time and effort to organize a party like that and then getting her to come to it? It's a bigger deal than most people realize."

She lifts her palms in the air in protest.

"Again, pure speculation. My own personal opinion," she says.

"So you think maybe he was throwing her the party as a way to make up for something?" I think back to the job offer in Kansas City. Maybe the party was more of a goodbye party than anything else?

Holly shrugs, practically lifting her shoulders to her ears. "I don't know. But my gut says there's more to it, that it wasn't a simple birthday celebration."

"Do you think she and Rob were having problems?"

She shakes her head. "I never got that impression, no. But anything can happen behind closed doors. That, and I'm the last person Celia would ever confide in about something like that."

True. My sister is a guarded person. The last thing she'd do is tell the town gossip about any marital discord.

"You want me to call Deirdre?" Holly asks. "Maybe I can FaceTime her."

"Who's Deirdre again?" I pull the folded list from my pocket and find her name somewhere toward the end.

"Our hairstylist," she says. "Everyone tells her everything all the time. She might know something I don't?"

Before I can process what's going on, she's tapping buttons on her phone screen and propping it up so we're both in view.

"Hello?" Deirdre's face fills the screen. "Holly, what's going on?"

"Hey, Deirdre—I'm here with Celia's sister Genevieve," she says.

"Hi." I lean closer until my face is in full view.

"She wants to know if there's anything we can think of that Celia might have been upset about recently," Holly says. "I told her about the pill thing."

I stiffen and bite my tongue.

The pill thing.

My sister has been missing a day and a half, and already Holly's spreading pillhead rumors. By the time this gets around town, people will be saying she's secretly away at some Malibu rehab center.

"Here's the thing," Deirdre says, messing with her hair and sweeping her bangs to the side, as if she can't help but use the phone camera as a mirror. "When people are in my chair, they tend to open up. They tell me things like . . . like I'm a therapist. I don't know what it is. If it's the intimate proximity and just being able to sit with someone and do nothing but talk for two straight hours? Whatever it is, people tend to spill their deepest secrets. I always joke that there's an attorney-client privilege thing going on, that whatever they say in the chair stays in the chair."

I adjust my posture, resting my chin on my hand and leaning in. Surely she knows something.

"That said," Deirdre continues, "out of all of my clients, Celia was never one to overshare."

I exhale, deflated.

"That also being said," Deirdre adds, "up until the party, I hadn't seen Celia in five weeks. She's actually on my books to come in next Friday. But I did see Isabel Delvy the week before last. The girl has more hair than she knows what to do with, so her appointments take forever. She showed up late. Over twenty minutes late. And she threw a bit of a fit when I wanted to rebook her. I ended up taking her, but the appointment was rushed. Anyway, the entire time she wanted to talk about Celia. She kept wanting to know what was new with her and when the last time I saw her was and all of this. And I told her those were interesting questions for someone who isn't friends with someone anymore. Isabel got upset and left as soon as I finished her cut. She slammed some cash on the counter and left, wet hair and all."

I can absolutely imagine Isabel doing something like that.

Holly groans. "*So* Isabel."

"I know the two of them had a falling-out," Deirdre says. "But it was my understanding that Isabel was the one who ended the friend-ship—so why was she so concerned about what Celia was up to?"

I exchange a look with Holly, who seems to be just as perplexed as everyone else.

"Do you have any idea why Isabel cut my sister out of her life?" I ask.

"Nope, not a clue. I briefly brought it up to Celia last time she was in, and she shut it down, saying Isabel just needed time to cool off. And then she started telling me about this girls' trip she and Natalie were plan-ning. She wanted me to come along, but I can't find a sitter for that week for my kids. Plus my schedule is insane because I just came back from a training in Miami. Anyway, that's all I really know. And I don't know if that's much of anything. Sometimes friendships just . . . fall out . . ."

This is true.

I've had enough friendships over the years to know that some-times they're as fickle as they are delicate, like an exotic houseplant that requires constant maintenance. The perfect amount of water. The right amount of light. If the pH of the soil is off by a decimal point in the wrong direction, it'll shrivel up and die overnight.

At least that's been my experience.

I imagine I'm not the only one.

"That said . . . people talk in this town," Deirdre continues, speak-ing lower and moving her face closer to the camera. "And someone who works at the hospital with Isabel and Rob—"

"Isabel works with Rob?" I interrupt. This is news to me.

Deirdre nods. "She works in HR, same office as Rob and everything."

"Okay," I say, "so what did you hear?"

She flattens her palm in front of her face. "Take this with a grain of salt, okay? Because people say a lot of things that aren't true—you know how that goes. Anyway, someone told me that Isabel had been spending a lot of time in Rob's office earlier this year and that just so happened to coincide with the falling-out Isabel and Celia had. The timeline lines up, if you know what I mean."

"So you think Rob was cheating on my sister with her best friend?" I've always felt Rob was too charismatic for his own good, and there's no denying he's an attractive man. If this is true, I can't say I'm surprised, but an HR executive spending time in the office of a hospital administrator isn't exactly damning evidence.

"I'm not saying I think that," she clarifies. "I'm just saying that someone told me that. That's all I know, and that's all I'm going to say."

She lifts her hand once more, as if to separate herself from the information she just relayed.

"Tell her about the fight," Holly says.

Deirdre claps her hands over her mouth. "Oh, my God. How could I forget?"

"What?" I ask, turning to Holly before meeting Deirdre's wild gaze on the screen. "What fight?"

"A couple of months back, I was at a little get-together at Monique Denman's, and someone said they overheard Celia and Isabel having some kind of heated exchange outside on the back patio," she says. "Now, I didn't see this myself. But another guest at the party said there was a broken wineglass involved and Celia left in tears."

She throws her hands up once more.

"And that's all I know," she adds.

"Who saw them fighting?" I ask.

Deirdre's lips press flat. "I don't know, sweetheart. I didn't know many people at the party. It was one of those things where someone is selling candles or leggings or whatever and they invite anyone with a pulse. I went because Monique is a client and she's always supported my business, so I wanted to return the favor. There were a lot of unfamiliar faces that night; that's all I remember."

"Wow. Okay. Well . . . thank you so much for sharing that," I say. "If you think of anything else, please let me know."

"Will do," she says. "Bye, Holly . . . see you Thursday at nine thirty."

Holly gives her a wave on camera before pressing the red button.

"What's your take on the Isabel situation?" I ask.

She brushes her hair from her shoulders, tugs the hem of her shirt down an inch or so, and then folds her arms.

"I honestly don't know," she finally says. "I've always kept a careful distance from that woman. There's just something about her that rubs me the wrong way, and I've never been able to put my finger on it."

"Same."

"You too?" She leans closer, and if I were the bonding type, I'd say this classifies as a bonding moment. Maybe this is how she gets people to open up so easily.

"She seemed unnaturally attached to my sister—at least whenever I was around them." I don't mention all the times I've seen them around town together because those instances were purely coincidental and the last thing I need is for Holly to twist the narrative and make me sound like a jealous sister-stalker. This bona fide gossip queen seems honest enough, but I'd rather not risk opening that can of worms. "Anyway, we could sit here and speculate all day, but I don't want to impose any more than I already have."

Nor do I want to perpetuate any rumors—not yet.

I rise from the table and collect my things.

"Thank you so much, Holly, for talking with me today," I say.

She walks me to the door, assuring me she'll call me the second she hears anything new.

I'm backing out of the driveway when I catch a glimpse of her pacing the living room, her phone pressed against her ear.

If I were the kind to pray these days, I'd pray that somebody somewhere knows something.

CHAPTER 22

GENEVIEVE

Present day

I collapse on our thrift store sofa Sunday evening, exhaustion wearing into my bones and my eyes so tired they cross if I focus on something across the room.

"Hey, Mom." Charlie saunters from the hallway, sliding her phone into the back pocket of her shorts. "I thought that was you."

She takes a seat beside me, but before I get a chance to appreciate it, my bedroom door swings open, and out walks my husband.

"Oh, hey," Brad says, a half-empty beer bottle in hand. "Was wondering when you were coming home."

He was wondering . . . but apparently not enough to pick up the phone.

My husband plants himself in his go-to recliner, and in a rare blink-and-I'll-miss-it moment, they both gift me their undivided attention.

This is . . . unnatural.

"Did you two miss me today or something?" I ask.

"Something like that," Brad says with a wink. He's never been good at sharing any kind of emotion, not that I have much room to talk.

Maybe that's why we worked so well together in the early years: we had a ridiculous amount of sex, and we also had an emotional understanding. We didn't talk about how we felt, and we didn't need fancy displays of affection to know we were committed to one another.

These days I feel like the very thing that worked for us from the start has now backfired in our faces.

"Did you have dinner yet?" I ask.

"Dad ordered pizza," Charlie volunteers.

I bite my lip to keep from reminding them we have an abundance of frozen pizzas in the freezer. I picked them up last weekend at the store—five pies for ten dollars. Dinner doesn't get much cheaper than that.

At least they didn't starve, I guess . . .

"Did you find Aunt Celia?" my daughter asks.

Brad's gaze is trained on me.

I didn't realize either of them cared.

"No," I say. "But I talked to some of her friends today."

"And?" Brad asks.

"There are some theories floating around." I look to my husband. "Nothing with merit, though."

"Maybe Uncle Rob did it," Charlie says, blurting her accusation with the kind of casualness that could only come from a teenager. It catches me off guard for a moment. And then I remind myself Charlie and Rob have exchanged a total of maybe eight words—ever. He isn't exactly an adoring uncle, and she isn't exactly a textbook-perfect niece. There's no attachment there, and I doubt there ever will be.

"Why would you say that?" I ask, not because she's in trouble but because I'm curious.

"Isn't it, like, always the husband or whatever?" She shrugs, picking at a hangnail on her thumb. "Maybe Uncle Rob was having an affair or something. Remember my friend back in Cross Beach? Stacia Drake? Her mom was cheating on her dad with their personal trainer, and the dad killed her, the other guy, and himself."

Brad and I exchange looks.

"You were only nine years old when that happened," Brad says. "You remember all of that?"

"It was all anyone was talking about for months. And Stacia moved away to live with her grandma in Boca Raton. How could I not remember my best friend moving away because her parents got murdered?"

Children are more observant, more aware of what's going on, than we give them credit for. I thought we did a decent job of sheltering her from that horrific tragedy. We kept the news off whenever she was in earshot, we never discussed it in front of her, and we'd always ask her how she was doing. She'd never talk about the Drakes, but she was still soaking everything in like a sponge outside the home.

"Do you think about that often?" I ask.

"No," she says. "Not really. Only when I'm around my friends' dads . . . I'm always wondering in the back of my mind if they're going to go crazy and murder someone."

"Even Callie's dad? And Eva's? They seem like lovely people," I say. When we moved here two years back, she was so worried she wouldn't meet any new friends. By the end of the first day of school, she had two. By the end of the week, she had an entire group of girlfriends. Not that I'm surprised—she's the opposite of a wallflower in every way.

She didn't get it from me.

"Stacia's dad was a *lovely* person, too," she says, using air quotes.

"This is true," Brad says, pointing the lip of his beer bottle our way. "The guy coached T-ball and soccer, and he was always loading Stacia and her friends up in his Escalade and taking them to trampoline parks and movies. Never would've thought in a million years he'd be the kind to snap."

"So what does any of this have to do with Uncle Rob?" I turn to my daughter.

She lifts a shoulder. "I don't know . . . I just don't like him, I guess. But maybe that's because I feel like he doesn't like us. He just seems, like, fake. That's the only way I can describe it. Like he's too nice. And too friendly. And he can turn on a smile like *that*."

She snaps her fingers. "Kinda gives me the creeps if I'm being honest," she adds.

I won't discredit her feelings about Rob, and I don't disagree with her either. I've always felt he was resentful of Celia's generosity to us. Letting us live in their rental home for free is huge. I tried to talk her out of it, insisting we wanted to contribute something. She merely shrugged and said as long as we covered the utilities, they'd take care of the rest.

I remember that conversation clear as day, too. It was here, in this very living room. And after they left, I watched Rob's face turn a shade of cherry red the second they got in his silver Lexus. Based on hand gestures and body language, it was clear their exchange was heated.

Sometimes, though, I wonder if it's the generosity that bothers him . . . or the fact that he swept her away from Cross Beach—only for her to bring a piece of Cross Beach here.

Is that why he wants to move her to Kansas City?

Is this a power move?

A control thing?

My phone buzzes on the coffee table.

Speak of the devil.

"Rob, hi," I answer in the middle of the first ring. My cheeks flush as if I've just been caught gossiping, despite the fact that he can't see them. "What's going on?"

"The police pinpointed her ticket," he says, breathless. The slam of a car door follows next. My heart bangs inside my chest before lurching up the back of my throat.

"Did they find her?" I ask, growing winded myself.

"No," he says. "But her last bank transaction was at the Metro-North station. Based on the amount she spent, we think she may have booked a round-trip ticket into Manhattan."

"Oh, my God." I rake my fingers through the hair at my temple. "You think she's in the city?"

"I don't know." The ding of his ignition follows. "I'm heading there now."

"Aren't the police going to search for her?"

"Schofield PD isn't going to send their manpower into a city of millions, trying to find a woman who left of her own free will." His tone is laced in annoyance. "But they've sent her picture to all of the precincts down there. I figured I'd head up and go to all our favorite haunts. The restaurants, the shops she loves, the neighborhoods. I know I'm looking for a needle in a haystack here, but I can't sit around at home waiting anymore."

"Do you want me to go with you?"

"No," he says. "Stay home. Be with your family. I'll let you know if I find her."

The call goes dead.

Why wouldn't he want me to help him look for her?

"What was that about?" Brad takes a swig of beer, his forehead creased.

"Rob says they think she's in Manhattan," I tell him and Charlie. "Based on the amount she spent, they think it was a round-trip ticket."

"This is good, right? It means she intends on coming back at some point, yeah?" Brad asks before tossing back the remainder of his IPA.

I place my phone facedown on the coffee table and exhale, letting the long day's work fade into the background.

"God, I hope so," I say, wondering again if Rob's insistence that I stay home had less to do with me spending time with my family and more to do with him trying to hide something now that the police have a confirmed location.

Celia is many things, but she's not someone who would want people sitting around worried sick about her, at least not people she cares about.

I think of all the voice mails I've left her, letting her know we're concerned, begging her to call me back. It's been almost two days now—she wouldn't leave people hanging for two days. Least of all her own husband.

Then again, she clearly needed to be gone for a bit, and given our track record, I'm the last person she'd confide in because she'd expect me to tell someone.

But I'm not the young girl I once was.

I can keep a secret with the best of them now.

"I should call Celeste." I rise from the sofa and swipe my phone off the coffee table. I've been putting off this call because I was hoping Celia would be back by now, that this whole thing was some kind of misunderstanding or false alarm. I don't know that Celeste will care, but given that they're sisters, she ought to know—assuming my father hasn't already told her. Though I doubt he cared enough to relay the news.

In his eyes, the Celia he loved died the day she left Cross Beach.

I shut myself in the bedroom, perch on the foot of the bed, and make the call.

"Hey, hey," she answers on the third ring, chipper as ever. "What's up?"

"So I have some strange news," I say, unsure if I'm choosing the right words.

She chuckles. "Um, okay."

"Have you talked to Dad lately?" I ask first.

Celeste sucks in a breath. "No, why? Is he okay?"

"Yeah, yeah, he's fine. I just . . . Celia is gone."

Silence settles between us.

"Gone?" she finally asks.

"Yeah." I slump over, brushing my free hand through my messy hair. "I guess she went for a drive or something in the middle of the night after her birthday party, and now they think she's in New York, but no one's been able to reach her."

"Hm. That *is* strange." She doesn't say a word beyond that. And I get it. What could she say? She doesn't know Celia, not in a traditional sense. She hardly remembers her. "Is there anything I can do? Do you want me to come look for her or something?"

The idea of Celeste boarding a flight to look for a sister who didn't even want her to attend her birthday party is bittersweet irony.

"No," I say. "That's not why I was calling. I just thought you should know."

I don't even think she could sniff her out of a lineup if she tried. It's been too long, and all she has to go off are fuzzy memories and faded childhood photographs.

Celeste exhales into the phone. "Does Dad know?"

"Yeah. I told him." There's no need to elaborate. We both know how he feels about her.

"I feel like I should be there," she says after a long pause. "I mean, if anything . . . I should be there for you. You must be beside yourself."

Over the past two years, I haven't gone into great detail with Celeste about anything up here. All she knows is that I came here to get close to Celia again, to get to know her again. And as far as she knows, it's all gone swimmingly. While it would've been easy to call Celeste and vent my frustrations at the fact that Celia is just as out of reach here as she's always been . . . I kept my feelings to myself.

It felt wrong to involve Celeste, to discolor her opinion on a sister she hasn't had a chance to get to know yet.

"Are you eating?" she asks. "Are you sleeping? Do you need help with Charlie?"

"Yeah, no, I'm fine. Everything's fine," I say. "It's all been a bit of a blur, but we're hanging in there."

"You sure you don't want me to come up for a few days?"

"I'm sure," I say. Celeste's job as a registered nurse at one of the busiest hospitals in the county doesn't offer her the kind of flexible schedule that would allow last-minute travel arrangements. And when she's not working, she's checking on Dad and Esta. There's no reason for her to come here.

Not yet.

I only hope that doesn't change.

CHAPTER 23

GENEVIEVE

Present day

I should have called out of work today—and I would have. But my paid time off accrues at a snail's pace, and it just so happens that I used the bulk of what I had last month when Charlie needed an emergency appendectomy.

I adjust my headset after returning from my morning break and make my system available for incoming calls. The phone rings in my ear, and I press the answer button.

"Eastward Telecom, this is Genevieve, how may I help you?" I ask in my most uplifting tone. I'm phoning it in today—no pun intended. But if I'm being honest, I phone it in every day. Though today there's a distinct detachment from reality. Physically I'm here. Mentally I'm somewhere else completely.

The elderly gentleman on the phone tells me his internet is down, but when I look up his account, I see that he's calling from his home phone, which is Voice over IP. He wouldn't be able to call me if his internet were truly offline.

"One moment, sir. I'm going to place you on a brief hold while I transfer you to tech support," I say.

I tried to work in tech support six months ago, when a spot opened up. The money was slightly better—$3.25 more an hour—so I figured it was worth a shot. They placed me there on a trial basis, but by the end of the first day, I was already begging to go back to my original position. The phone calls would inevitably end in tears more often than not—on both sides—and management wasted no time putting me back in the central call center.

A second call comes through—a woman questioning the new $4.34 universal service charge Eastward Telecom has recently implemented on all accounts.

"Yes, ma'am, I understand you didn't authorize that charge." I keep my voice calm and even keeled, like a dead-inside Disney employee. "We sent out a notice last month to all of our customers, giving them a heads-up about the new charge. Perhaps you saw it? It was printed on yellow paper, about the size of a postcard."

"I want this fee removed. I didn't consent," she says, clearly not understanding me. This happens from time to time; customers get so frustrated, they aren't capable of processing the words I'm saying.

"Unfortunately I'm unable to remove the universal surcharge." I place some manufactured sympathy in my delivery. "This is a company-wide change, affecting all accounts."

The woman screams a string of profanities into the phone before slamming the receiver. At least she didn't ask to speak to my manager, who is nearly impossible to reach since he's always gallivanting around the office making idle chitchat.

I tap the button on my screen to make myself unavailable for a moment, and then I check my phone for the millionth time today. I've been watching it all morning, waiting to hear from Rob. I've called and texted him a couple of times, but I've yet to receive a response.

I've also reached out to both Monique Denman and Isabel Delvy.

My original plan was to go straight down the list of names Rob gave me, speaking with each and every birthday party guest to try to glean any speck of information I could, but I can't stop thinking about what Celia's hairdresser said about Isabel and the fight at Monique's.

I readjust my headset and hover my mouse over the available button. We're required to average ten calls per hour, minimum, and sitting out for too long can affect my average. Those who reach their averages get bonuses each pay period. It's an extra hundred bucks, but that kind of money adds up for a paycheck-to-paycheck family like us.

I take another call—this one from a senior man wanting to add long distance to his plan. I make his day when I tell him it's already included. Whoever sold him the original package last month didn't explain that to him, so he's been holding off on making any long-distance calls, fearing he'd have to pay fifteen cents a minute.

The next call that comes through is from a woman wanting to make a payment on her past-due account before it gets shut off. I process her payment with poise and genuine sympathy, because I've been there a time or two (or three).

For the next two hours, I operate on autopilot, taking calls, helping customers, and maintaining my "phone voice." When it's time for lunch, I clock out, hop in my car, and drive around town eating the peanut butter sandwich and string cheese I packed for lunch. This is usually the highlight of my day . . . aimlessly driving through Schofield, listening to music, no one bothering me, no one screaming in my ear.

Only on this particular day, I'm not cruising around taking a joyride.

I head straight to Rob and Celia's house.

I've no intention of bothering him—I just want to see if he's home.

I want to know if I'm being ignored and avoided . . . or if he's still in the city looking for my sister.

Turning down their tree-lined street, I cruise past inquisitive neighbors and dog walkers, past stroller-pushing, power walking mamas and a postal worker delivering a package. When I get to the last house on the left, I gasp.

Rob's shiny silver Lexus is resting in the driveway.

He's home.

Which means he's ignoring me.

Why?

Without thinking twice, I jerk my steering wheel and pull in behind him, blocking his car should he try to leave. Dashing up the front walk, I make it to the door only slightly out of breath, and I press the doorbell no less than three times.

A minute later, Rob answers.

The dark circles under his eyes and the crestfallen look on his face tell me he didn't find my sister.

"I've been calling you all morning," I say.

"Yeah, sorry." He runs his fingers through his messy hair. When I take a step back and get a good look at him, I realize he's in sweats and a T-shirt. "I was up all night looking for her, came back this morning, and crashed for a couple of hours. I was just getting ready to call you, actually."

Now I feel bad; that is, if he's telling the truth.

"You mind explaining this?" He hands me a piece of stationery with some sort of vintage floral pattern along the top. In the middle are the words **YOU DON'T DESERVE ANY OF THIS** along with **JUNE 14th** circled and underscored twice.

"What . . . where did this come from?" I hand it back. "What is this?"

"Found it in a stack of birthday cards from Friday night."

"I've never seen that in my life."

"Whoever wrote this obviously wanted to upset her."

"That's really messed up . . . Do you think—is it possible this is what set her off?"

"You can drop the act, Genevieve." He braces an arm on the doorjamb, as if to imply that I'm not welcome inside.

"What are you saying?"

"Whoever wrote this was clearly jealous of her," he says. "They wanted to ruin her special night."

"What are you saying?" I ask again, this time enunciating each and every syllable.

"I think you know exactly what I'm saying."

"Why would I want to upset my sister on her birthday? What would I get out of that?" It doesn't make sense. Celia has done nothing but help me and my family in the two years since we reconnected. Why would I want to hurt her in return?

"Oh, I don't know . . . some kind of sick satisfaction?" His face is pinched, and his eyes glint with hatred. "From the moment we moved you here, you've been jealous of her. That's why she's had such a difficult time reconnecting. Being around you makes her feel guilty, though for what I can't imagine. She walked through fire to get to where she is, and she owes none of it to you."

My jaw would hit the ground if it weren't so clenched. *"Rob."*

If I made her feel guilty, it was never intentional. All the times I complained to her about my husband or mentioned that money was tight, I was simply venting to my older sister, not inadvertently asking her for handouts or hoping she'd throw another generous bone our way. I was only ever trying to bond with her.

"You resented her for getting out of Cross Beach," he continues. "You resented her for leaving you behind. You resented her for having the audacity to go against your parents, because you never could. You resent this life she's built . . . this happy home, a loving marriage, more friends than she knows what to do with. She's fulfilled, and she doesn't have to want for anything, and you can't stand it."

Spittle flies from his tight lips, and a vein pulses across his forehead.

"I get that you're frustrated and angry, but I'm telling you I'm—"

He cuts me off. "Something in her changed the minute we moved you here." A flush creeps from his neck upward, until his entire face is mottled and splotched an angry shade of red. "She started having nightmares again, stopped sleeping, started pulling away from me when I'd ask her what was wrong."

"So that's *my* fault?"

"She wasn't like this before, that's all I know."

The boldness of his accusations cuts through me like an obsidian knife—sharp and clean. This explains his phony facade around us, that fake disappearing smile Charlie mentioned. The gut feeling that always accompanies his presence.

He doesn't want us here.

He never did.

"Is this why you applied for that job in Kansas City?" I turn the tables.

His brows meet. "What the hell are you talking about?"

"You wanted to move her away . . . from me."

An incredulous expression colors his face.

"Go back to Cross Beach where you belong, Genevieve." His tone is low yet firm, like a man who means business. "I want you and your family out of that house by the end of the month."

The abrupt slamming of the door is followed by the snick of the dead bolt.

I didn't even get a chance to ask him about the Isabel affair rumors.

Just like that, Rob locks me out of his life.

Though perhaps that's what he wanted all along . . .

CHAPTER 24

Genevieve

Twenty-seven years ago

"What color do you want your skirt to be?" I show my sister the drawing I made of us. "I was thinking pink with purple stripes."

"You pick," Celia says with a smile as she dips her spoon into her mint chip ice cream.

I finished mine first, practically inhaling it, but like always, Celia's made hers last three times longer.

"We better wipe that chocolate off your face before your parents see it." Our babysitter, Alison, runs a damp paper towel across my mouth and chin. "Must destroy all evidence . . ."

The first Friday of each month, Alison babysits us so my parents and her parents can have dinner with the pastor, his wife, and another couple from church.

"They'd throw a fit if they knew we walked to the gas station," she says with a rebellious glint in her eye. While my parents have strict rules about not leaving the house, not answering the door, and not watching TV while she's here, Alison always finds a way to bend those rules without getting caught.

"Can I braid your hair?" Celia asks Alison before turning to me. "Gen, you can braid mine if you want."

"Go for it." Alison takes a seat on the floor, in front of the sofa, and Celia climbs behind her. "Gen, can you grab some hair ties for us?"

I skip to the bathroom, grab a few elastics, and return to the living room, scooching next to Alison.

"Can I tell you guys a secret?" Alison asks.

"Of course," Celia says as I get situated behind her.

I lean close, my ears practically on fire.

"I have a boyfriend." Alison giggles, clamping her hand over her mouth before her expression morphs into something serious. She points at each of us. "Do *not* tell anyone, okay? My parents would literally kill me if they knew."

I've never thought of Mrs. and Mr. Lang as the murderous type, but if they're anything like our parents, they wouldn't be happy about it, that's for sure.

"Are you even old enough to have a boyfriend?" I scratch my temple and do some quick math. I'm pretty sure she's only seventeen, last I checked. My parents told us we can't even court someone until we're out of high school, and it has to be someone of their liking.

"What's his name?" Celia asks before Alison has a chance to answer my question.

"Celia," I say, scolding her. She shouldn't be so nosy. Our parents always say other people's business is none of ours and vice versa.

"It's a secret," Alison fires back without hesitation. A slow smile claims her mouth, and her eyes are nothing but stars and light. I've never seen her this excited about anything in all the years we've known her.

"What's he look like?" Celia asks.

"Celia," I scold her again.

"Gen, isn't it past your bedtime?" my sister interjects.

"It's actually past both of your bedtimes." Alison's never been one to play favorites.

"All right, all right. I'm almost done." Celia wraps an elastic around the bottom of Alison's french braid. I haven't even started hers. Maybe she'll let me do her hair tomorrow? "There."

"Okay, girls, off to bed." Alison rises from the floor and points to the hall. "Your parents are going to be home any minute."

This is always the worst part of the night—when the fun is officially over. It's like that Cinderella story when the carriage turns back into a pumpkin. Our evenings with Alison are always magical, and the instant my parents step foot back inside the house, all that magic fades away.

"See you at church," Alison says when she tucks me in. "Remember—we never walked to the gas station for ice cream, and I don't have a boyfriend."

She winks.

I run my fingers across my lips, pretending to zip them.

Her secrets are always safe with me.

Not two minutes pass before I hear the two of them talking in Celia's room, their voices carrying through the paper-thin walls that divide us.

Can't remember the last time Celia and I whispered and giggled.

I bury my head under my pillow, squeeze my eyes tight, and ignore the liquid-hot jealousy burning through me.

CHAPTER 25

GENEVIEVE

Present day

"Monique? Hi, this is Genevieve Jacobs—Celia's sister." I phone Monique on the way back to work after leaving Rob's, now more determined than ever to keep my foot in the door of this investigation.

"Genevieve, yes, hi," she says, slightly breathless. There's some kind of commotion behind her that I can't make out.

"Is now a good time?"

"I'm just checking on a remodel job for one of my clients, but I have a few minutes. Why? What's going on? Have they found her yet?"

I come to a stop at a busy intersection and take a deep breath.

"Not yet," I say. "We're still looking, but I had some questions I was hoping you could answer?"

"Of course. What do you need to know?"

The light flicks to green.

"I spoke to Holly and Deirdre," I say, "and they mentioned something about Celia and Isabel getting into some kind of fight at your party a couple months back?"

Monique is silent, though the ruckus on her end is louder than ever.

"Let me step outside, hang on," she finally says. A minute later, she clears her throat. "Now, I . . . I don't like to gossip or insinuate things."

"I would never want you to do that. I'm just trying to get a better idea of what happened."

"All I know is that the two of them stepped outside, and my sister-in-law said she heard them say something about *marriage*. Next thing she knew, Isabel was throwing a wineglass, and Celia was leaving in tears."

"So you don't know what the fight was over?"

"Not at all," she says. "But later that night, Celia called to apologize. She was embarrassed, understandably. And the next day, Isabel showed up at my door with a brand-new set of stemware. I asked each of them if everything was okay, and neither wanted to say much. They sort of brushed it off, and I didn't feel it was my place to pry. It was clearly a personal and private conversation. I wish I had more information for you."

"Do you still keep in touch with Isabel?" I ask.

"I haven't seen or heard from her since the day she showed up with the wineglasses," Monique says. "I imagine she's still a little embarrassed. I know I would be . . . That sort of scene doesn't really happen around here, and it's all anyone could talk about for weeks after."

"Strange."

"Yes, very," she says. "Anyway, I hate to cut this short, but my clients are here and we're about to do a progress walk-through, so I need to let you go. But please call me if you need anything else, all right?"

I hang up with Monique and drive back to the office. But before I head inside, I call Isabel and leave a message telling her it's imperative that she return my call as soon as possible.

I have questions.

And evidently she's the one with the answers.

CHAPTER 26

Genevieve

Present day

I stand before the glossy black entrance of 377 Corcoran Drive—the residence of Isabel and Grant Delvy—shortly after six o'clock Monday evening.

I came straight from work, hoping to catch Isabel in person since she's been dodging my calls and texts all day. I'm seconds from pressing the antique brass doorbell when I hear the raucous symphony of a marital argument—a sound I'm unfortunately too familiar with.

Leaning in, I all but press my ear against the door, trying to make out the words coming from inside.

"This is what you wanted, wasn't it?" the male asks.

"Not like this," the female—Isabel, I assume—replies.

The sound of shattering glass follows—fitting, given the argument she had with my sister two months ago. Celia has never been violent or hot tempered. She's as cool and collected as they come, even in the most emotionally charged moments.

"Maybe you can pay for it with that twenty-five grand," the man says.

"See? This is why . . ." Isabel says, her words drowned out by heavy footsteps.

"This isn't why and you know it." His voice is louder than before. Closer.

I press the doorbell, hoping to break up whatever's going on inside because it's escalating by the second. Their fight turns into heavy silence. An endless second later, the door swings open, and standing before me is a disheveled Isabel with black mascara stains beneath her bloodshot eyes.

I steal a glimpse past her shoulder, noticing a packed suitcase by the bottom of the stairs as well as a smashed vase and trampled red roses.

"Hi . . ." I say. "Everything okay in there?"

Her bottom lip trembles, and her eyes turn glassy. "Now's not a good time, Genevieve."

"Now is a perfect time." A handsome man with a runner's build and jet-black hair grabs the rolling suitcase at the bottom of the stairs, stepping over the mess of broken glass, water, and wilting scarlet flower petals. "I was just leaving."

"Grant," Isabel calls to her husband as he squeezes past her. I stand out of the way as he lugs his suitcase over the threshold. "Wait."

He ignores her, his long legs carrying him away from the house by the second.

She swipes at a tear, then folds her arms.

"I've been trying to reach you all day," I say. "I was hoping I could catch you after work . . . I just have some questions about Celia."

"I've been a little"—her eyes flick over my shoulder, where her husband is throwing his luggage into the trunk of his graphite-gray Maserati—"preoccupied."

"I'm so sorry," I say.

Her attention returns to me, her gaze running the length of my body, from head to toe and back, as if she doesn't believe me. But I am sorry. I don't wish for anyone to go through marital struggles.

"I'm sure you've heard about Celia?" I ask.

She waves for me to come in. "Of course I have."

Isabel shuts the door behind me before disappearing into the kitchen. She returns with a broom, dustpan, garbage pail, and roll of paper towels. Crouching down, she cleans up the mess at the bottom of the stairs.

I kneel beside her, carefully plucking large shards of glass and dropping them in the trash.

"I've been talking to some of her closest friends," I say with a careful tone. I don't want to put her on the defensive. "Everyone keeps mentioning the two of you had a recent falling-out . . . that there was some kind of fight . . . and there are rumors about you and Rob . . ."

Isabel chuffs, her lips curling at one side. She sweeps a mountain of broken glass into the dustpan.

"So because we're no longer friends," she says, "you think I had something to do with her disappearance."

"No," I say. "Not at all. I was just wondering if you could tell me what actually happened? Apparently she refused to tell anyone about it, not even Rob."

Isabel dumps the glass in the bin, and it lands with a heavy clink.

"Makes sense," she says.

"What do you mean?"

"I'm sorry, Genevieve, but if Celia wasn't comfortable talking to her own husband about what happened, I don't feel that it's my place to share it with you."

Even on the outs, her loyalty doesn't waver.

Impressive.

"We think something upset her Friday night, after her birthday party, and I'm trying to determine what that is." I don't mention the note, not yet. "Rob said he invited you to the party."

"I wanted to go," she says. "It just . . . wasn't a good idea."

"What do you mean?"

Isabel carries the trash bin back to the kitchen, and I follow with the broom and dustpan.

"Perhaps it wasn't obvious enough a moment ago, but my husband and I are currently going through something." A rivulet of blood drips down her left ring finger, and I can't help but notice she isn't wearing a wedding band.

"You're bleeding." I point.

Isabel sighs before running her hand under cold water and grabbing a towel. "Of course."

"You need to put pressure on it," I say as the blood soaks through the towel. "You must've been nicked pretty good."

"So what is it you needed from me? Exactly?" She changes the subject, her wounded hand wrapped tight and pressed against her stomach. "Other than asking why our friendship ended . . ."

"Have you tried to contact her at all? Since your fight?"

"We didn't have a *fight*." She angles her chin. "We had a misunderstanding."

"Must have been quite the misunderstanding if you ended a friendship over it." I don't mention the part about her smashing a wineglass at Monique's party.

I brace myself for a snarky comeback, an Isabel witticism, only instead I'm met with an unexpected waterfall of tears and a slumping Isabel burying her head in her hands.

Is she acting?

Is this theatrics?

Is she overcompensating for something?

I'm frozen on the other side of her quartz island, unsure of how to comfort her or if I should even bother. She's never liked me, I've never liked her, and now here we are. I doubt she wants my comfort any more than I want to offer it.

"Isabel, please," I say. "Tell me what happened. I'm worried about my sister. I need to find her. I need her to come home."

She swipes at her tears with the back of her un-nicked hand.

"I have no idea where she is or where she would have gone," she says, her voice broken. "I actually tried calling her yesterday, when I first found out she was gone. I got her voice mail, but I left a message hoping she'd call me."

"We think she's in New York City," I say. "Do you know if she'd have any reason to go there?"

Isabel's gaze grows distant, and she seems to be lost in thought for a moment.

"No," she finally answers. "She and Rob would go into the city once a month for fun, but other than that . . ."

My altercation with Rob earlier today has been playing on a loop in my mind for hours, the way it happened out of nowhere, the way he turned on me so quickly, the way he wanted to pin this entire thing on me with no proof beyond a piece of paper—a piece of paper he could have manufactured himself for all anyone knows. Not to mention, I wasn't even at the party that night. How would I have slipped something in with her gifts, unseen?

"Do you know if she and Rob were having any problems?" I ask. "She never really talked to me about those sort of things . . ."

Isabel rolls her eyes, her lashes damp and jet black. "Don't get me started on Rob."

"What do you mean?"

"He doesn't deserve her," she says.

Interesting choice of words . . .

"Celia is a kept woman. We all know that, right?" Isabel asks. "But that's only because Rob wants her that way. If you ask me, he likes that she's completely, one hundred percent emotionally and financially dependent on him. She couldn't leave if she wanted to."

"Has she ever mentioned wanting to leave him?"

"Never." She shakes her head, her voice low. "Unfortunately."

"Care to elaborate?" This is all new to me.

Her lips tremble, and she checks her bleeding finger. "I . . . I was . . . I am . . . I'm in love with your sister."

"I'm sorry?" I must have misheard her.

"Celia and I fell out because I wanted more." Her voice is quiet, laced with a hint of shame or perhaps regret. "I kissed her. Earlier this year. We were on a girls' trip in Miami, sharing a hotel room. We'd had way too much to drink. I climbed into her bed and we were talking all night. It felt . . . intimate. More intimate than it usually felt. Something just came over me in that moment, and I kissed her."

A thick tear slides down her cheek.

"She kissed me back, Genevieve," she says. "The whole thing lasted maybe less than a minute, but she kissed me back. I didn't imagine it." Isabel rolls her eyes. "The next day she acted like nothing happened, and when I tried to bring it up, she said it was a mistake, that she drank too much. But even after we went home and back to our lives and our husbands, I couldn't stop thinking about her . . . in that way."

She tosses the bloody towel in the trash can.

"That moment we shared, it woke something inside of me that I never knew was there," Isabel continues. "I couldn't keep pretending like it never happened . . . like it was a mistake . . . So two months ago, I pulled Celia aside at Monique's party, told her I loved her, and kissed her again. That time she pulled away, told me I'd lost my mind, and . . . everything fell apart after that."

It makes sense now . . . her obsession with my sister, her blatant possessiveness.

She was in love with Celia. Consumed by her. She wanted her for herself.

It also makes sense why my sister wouldn't want to discuss this with her husband. In her eyes it was just a kiss that meant nothing.

"I'm worried about her." Isabel's voice shakes. "I wanted to see her Friday night. I wanted to go to the party—to surprise her. I was willing to settle for a friendship again as long as it meant having her in my life. But earlier that day, Grant found my credit card statement and saw I'd recently taken out a twenty-five-thousand-dollar cash advance."

That must be why he referenced that money during their spat earlier . . .

"I was planning on leaving him, and I needed money to retain a divorce attorney," she says. "Long story short, I came clean to him about my feelings for Celia . . . and before I could explain to him that those feelings weren't reciprocated, he flew into a blind rage."

My body tenses.

"Grant has always had a temper." Her voice shakes, and her eyes grow unfocused. "But this was unlike anything I'd ever seen before. He punched our bedroom door and hurled his wedding band at me, he screamed in my face, with this terrifying look in his eyes, and he called me the kind of names I'd never call my worst enemy."

"Isabel . . ."

"He left after that. He said he was going to stay in a hotel, but I don't know if he did or not. He cut off my access to our bank account. I just know that he left, and the next day . . . I found out Celia was gone."

I clamp my hand over my mouth, breathing through my fingers.

"Do you think he had something to do with . . . ?" I can't finish my thought.

Isabel buries her face in her hands again, her shoulders slumping, collapsed by the weight of this moment. "I don't know," she says. "I . . . don't think so? But I don't know."

"We should go to the police," I say.

Isabel shakes her head. "I can't."

"Why not?"

She lifts her hand, which is still bleeding profusely. "I should probably get this looked at. It's pretty deep."

She's right. It's showing no signs of slowing down.

"Come on, I'll drive you," I say.

I take Isabel to the urgent care center on Benton Avenue, and the moment they take her back, I step outside and call the Schofield Police Department, asking for Detective Samuels. They patch me through to his cell phone, and I tell him everything I know about Grant Delvy.

CHAPTER 27

GENEVIEVE

Present day

"What do you think?" I ask Brad as I climb into bed beside him, massaging a nickel-sized amount of cream onto the backs of my hands. From the moment I walked in the door this evening, I unloaded the entirety of my day on him, hardly pausing to catch my breath.

He sinks into the mattress, rolling to his side and facing me. "I think if you put half the effort into our marriage that you've been putting into this investigation, we'd be a hell of a lot happier than we are."

I have no words.

He rolls to his other side, reaching up to turn out the lamp. Darkness swallows the room. While I have half a mind to switch my lamp on and pick a fight, I don't have the energy.

Somewhere along the line, we both stopped caring.

The effort stopped cold.

It was as if someone slapped a do-not-resuscitate order on our marriage and neither of us noticed.

There's a deep and profound ache in my core when I realize I'm married to a man and I don't even know if he likes me. I don't remember the last time he looked at me the way Rob looks at Celia.

I can't remember the last time the two of us had a good laugh or sat through a dinner without an undercurrent of tension marring our idle conversation.

I flip the covers off my legs and make my way to Charlie's room. She was already in bed by the time I got home tonight. Even if she's too old to be tucked in and she's long stopped requiring bedtime stories and snuggles, I'd rather be with her tonight than lie next to my husband, thinking about all the ways we got off track.

Crawling in beside Charlie, I nuzzle up behind her, breathing in the sugar-sweet scent of her vanilla-berry body spray that perpetually wafts from her hair and skin and pillows and bedsheets. I gently wrap my arm around her, listen to her steady breath, and close my eyes.

For the hours that follow, I lie wide awake, marinating in my failure as a wife, as a mother, as a human being. I was so busy trying to do everything right that somewhere along the line I did everything wrong.

It's easy to blame Brad for being selfish and checked out, but I haven't exactly been engaged in the relationship either. I've settled for silence over nagging. I've stewed my anger until it simmers just beneath the surface, rather than expressing how I feel.

And with Charlie, I've been so wrapped up in being the doting mother I always wished I had that I molded her into the entitled teenager she is today. That, combined with her being my one shot at parenthood, has led me to overcompensate from every angle. Perhaps I've been so hell bent on being some unrealistic made-for-TV version of a mother that I commandeered the bulk of the parenting responsibilities. I am the nurturer *and* the disciplinarian. The car pool driver. The lunch lady. The sock darner. The bed maker. The homework helper. The one Charlie always goes to first for anything—leaving little to no use for Brad.

I can fix this.

It'll take work on all sides, but maybe there's hope for us after all.

I think of my sister and what she would do if she were me.

Celia has never been afraid of failure—that was always the biggest difference between us.

I've let fear dictate every decision I've ever made.

It ends now.

CHAPTER 28

Genevieve

Twenty years ago

"I have something for you." I pull my little sister aside and hand her a pink tea rose I picked from the bushes on the south side of the house. "Happy birthday, Celeste."

Her pale blue eyes widen as she reaches for the delicate little bloom, and then she wraps her arms tight around me.

"You're the *best* sister in the whole entire world." Celeste buries her head in my shoulder. While her words bathe my heart in warmth, they break it, too.

If only I had been a better sister to Celia, maybe she'd have stayed. Maybe she'd be with us right now.

Earlier today we went to church in true Fielding tradition so Celeste could praise God for giving her another year on this earth. We don't do birthday parties, cakes, candles, or presents, but I wanted to give her something special anyway—just like Celia used to do for me. It was always little things—a drawn picture or a shiny rock or a handmade hair bow. But I treasured them.

Today Celeste is six.

And today Celia is twenty . . . assuming she's still alive.

A little less than two years ago, she left. And we haven't seen or heard from her since. Not a call, not a letter, not a word. My parents received a message from her college saying she hadn't been attending classes. My father drove up to her dorm and spoke to her roommate, who said she hadn't seen her in at least two weeks. In fact, Celia had told her she was going home to take care of some personal matters. She'd left everything behind except for a few changes of clothes.

Just like that, Celia was gone.

"Thanks, Genevieve. It's beautiful." Celeste releases her hold on me before tucking the flower behind one ear and slipping her hand into mine. "Can you push me on the swing now?"

"It would be my honor, princess," I tease as she drags me to the swing set my father built for her in our backyard.

Celia and I never had a swing set when we were Celeste's age. My parents said it was a frivolous want and not a need, that our free time was better spent in prayer and devotion than ripping our dresses and skinning our knees on playground equipment.

In many ways, they've lightened up a little since Celeste came into our lives, but maybe that's because they view her as a literal gift from the heavens, from God himself.

Six years ago, my father was jogging past a nearby park early one morning when he heard a baby crying. He followed the sound to a plastic tunnel that connected one side of the playground to the other. Inside he found a newborn baby girl swaddled in a yellow blanket.

I'm not sure of the specifics after that. I know the department of human services got involved, and I remember my parents speaking to a social worker off and on in the weeks that followed. And the news wanted to interview my father. I think they were waiting to see if anyone would step up and claim her—but no one ever did.

Then one day, my parents brought her home and told us she was our new sister.

My father, supported by the entire church community, gave a compelling testimony about how he felt a connection to her, how he believed he was meant to find her that day, and how he wanted to raise her in "God's glory."

Within a year, she was legally adopted and officially the third Fielding daughter.

Everyone in town knows her as the Cimarron Park baby, and when she's old enough, my parents intend to sit her down and tell her the story of how she came to be a part of our family. But until then, she's our Celeste. Our heaven-sent ray of sunshine.

"Genevieve, the Jacobs family is here," Mom calls from the back door.

A thousand tiny butterflies swarm my stomach, and I fight the silly grin threatening to take over the bottom half of my face.

"Should we head in?" I ask Celeste.

"Just a few more pushes? Please?" She kicks her legs.

"Fine, but only because it's your birthday." I push her a few more times before gently guiding the swing to a standstill, and then we head inside to where Pastor Jacobs, his wife, and his oldest son, Brad, are waiting.

Our parents are arranging a courtship for Brad and me. Apparently he's had an eye for me over the years, though I was always oblivious—and knew better than to so much as think about crushing on a boy. Now that we're both eighteen and finished with high school, he thought it would be the right time to get to know me . . . with our parents' blessings, of course.

Celeste and I head inside, where everyone's gathered around the kitchen table, sipping sweet tea and making small talk.

My gaze scans to Brad before flicking to the floor when our eyes catch. My stomach somersaults a couple of times, and my cheeks flush with warmth, but I take a deep breath, tuck my hair behind my ear, and offer him a smile.

While I've known him practically my entire life, I never once thought he'd be the one I could potentially spend the rest of my life with. As the pastor's firstborn child and only son, he's practically royalty at our church. My parents couldn't be more thrilled about this entire thing.

"Hi, Genevieve," he says.

"Hi, Brad." I like the way his name feels on my lips, solid and unyielding. Kind of like the way he's built with his broad shoulders and hands that are good at fixing just about anything.

Sometimes when I'm lying in bed at night, I try to imagine the two of us married. Never mind the fact that we haven't even held hands yet. But either way, I can almost see it so perfectly clear. I always start with the wedding first—me in an ivory lace dress with a train that stretches all the way down the altar, and him in a navy-blue tux that matches his eyes. His father would conduct the ceremony—that's a given. And his mother would be sitting in the front row, next to mine, the two of them grinning, eyes filled with happy tears.

I think of our future children next. Will they get his dimpled smile? My wavy hair? Will they be tall and broad like him or average in height like me? What kind of father will Brad be? And what kind of mother will I be? Will we make time for joy and laughter, or will our lives be so consumed by the church that we don't have time for frivolities?

These are conversations I hope to have with Brad soon enough, when we can finally be alone and get to know each other better.

I plan to tell him I want a happy marriage, one with fewer constraints and a little more freedom. If I'm lucky, he'll want the same. But if he's just going to be another carbon copy of Jim Fielding, I'll have to pass. I respect my father's love for the church, but I don't think God would give us this life if we were only meant to spend it worshipping him. Surely he loves us enough to want us to be happy, too? Why would he give us the ability to feel joy if we weren't supposed to use it?

There's warmth in Brad's eyes when I steal a glimpse at him again.

He looks like he could be a soft place to land.

Something tells me we could be happy together.

CHAPTER 29

GENEVIEVE

Present day

"Genevieve?" A woman's voice calls my name as I gas up my car Tuesday morning before work. Shielding the sun from my eyes, I turn to find a vaguely familiar face. "Genevieve Jacobs?"

A dark-haired woman flags me down from behind her black sedan at the pump behind me, her gaze squinted and a smile painted on her red lips. "It's Melody . . ." she says. "Melody *Brunner*. We used to work together? Like a lifetime ago?"

The name registers before her face does, but now I remember.

I make my way toward her.

"Oh, gosh." I clap my hands over my heart before her lips spread into a mile-wide grin. I haven't seen her since my early days at Eastward Telecom. Melody took me under her wing, trained me, and gave me all the ins and outs. Then one day out of the blue, she quit without notice. Rumor was she met a man online and decided to pick up her entire life on a whim. "Mel, my goodness, it's been forever. I almost didn't recognize you. You cut your hair . . ."

My former cubicle mate throws her arms around me, squeezing me tight and depositing an obscene amount of her signature Dior Poison perfume on my shirt in the process. It's all coming back to me now.

"What are you doing back in Schofield?" I ask. "I thought you moved to Bridgeport?"

"I moved back about a year and a half ago," she says. "Didn't work out."

I'm not surprised, given the rumor, but I don't have time to pry. From what I recall, Melody is a talker, particularly when it comes to her romantic life. Lovely and friendly but doesn't pick up on social cues and always had a habit of oversharing every last detail. Brad used to joke that she used me as her human diary.

"So, what are you up to these days?" I ask, praying she gives a catchall answer.

"Little of this, little of that. Managing a little boutique on the square for now, waiting for something better to come along. How are things with your sister—Celia, right?" she asks.

I didn't share many personal details with her during our time together except for the fact that I'd moved here to reunite with my older sister—a small tidbit Melody apparently remembers.

"Oh, you know . . . everyone's so busy," I say. "But we see each other when we can."

Do I tell her Celia's currently missing in action? God forbid something happens to my sister and Melody's impeccable memory recalls the day she ran into me and I told her all was fine. I don't want to be misleading, but I also don't want to drop a bombshell like that in the middle of mindless small talk.

Then again, it feels wrong to pretend all is well when all is the opposite of well.

"Actually," I begin to say until my attention is stolen by an auburn-haired woman in a strappy floral sundress who looks eerily similar to my missing sister. My breath catches in my throat until I spot her retrieve a pair of Jackie O.–sized sunglasses from her purse. Celia would never wear anything like that.

The woman glances over her shoulder, almost as if she can sense she's being watched. And then she climbs into the driver's seat of a Porsche SUV. A moment later, the windows are rolled down and a bass-rattling techno song plays on full blast.

It isn't Celia.

"I'm so sorry, Gen," Melody says, pulling me back into the present moment. "I'm running late for an appointment, but it was great seeing you. Hope to run into you again sometime."

With a friendly smile, she places the gas nozzle back into the pump before ducking into her car.

By the time I glance up, the SUV with the Celia look-alike is long gone.

I climb into my car and check my phone, where an unread message from Celeste is waiting.

Any news with Celia? she writes.

You free for a chat? I type back.

Heading in for an extra shift right now. I'm off at six if you want to call me then? she replies.

The honk of a car horn behind me sends a start to my chest. In my rearview I spot a bald man in a two-seater convertible, anxious to use the pump I'm blocking. He makes some sort of gesture with his hands, mouthing words I can only imagine aren't all that kind.

I get out of the way, head to the office, and contemplate my next move.

CHAPTER 30

GENEVIEVE

Present day

"Any word from Grant?" I stop by Isabel's during my lunch hour Tuesday, mostly to check on her hand but also to see if anything has changed with her husband since last night. On the way home from the urgent care clinic, I told her I'd given his name to the detective on the case. She was upset—mostly worried about him potentially losing his dental practice should he be criminally charged—but at the same time she understood.

"I tried calling him today, just to make sure he was okay," she says. "But he sent me straight to voice mail. A minute later, he texted me with his attorney's name and number. He says all contact needs to go through his attorney from now on. That's what I get for caring, I guess."

Spiteful prick.

"I'm so sorry," I say. Whatever I may say about Brad, he's never thrown a vase at me, cut me off from our bank accounts, or called me names.

She chuffs. "The man's got a narcissistic streak a mile deep. He can't handle rejection of any kind. That's why his temper is so bad—'narcissistic rage' is what they call it. I didn't realize what he was until a couple of years into our marriage, when the love bombing stopped and the real Grant came out. We did counseling, and we were fine for a while . . . and then the whole thing with Celia happened this year, and it's like we're right back where we started. Only this time it looks like divorce is the only fix now. There's no saving this. And even if there were, there's nothing left to save. I don't love him, not anymore."

"Marriage is hard," I say. "It's not for everyone."

"I was thinking more about Celia and Rob last night," she says. "Maybe this is nothing, but for the past couple years or so, Celia would occasionally mention she felt like she was being watched or followed. Like she had a stalker or something."

"Really?" This is news to me.

"She'd get these hang-up phone calls at all hours of the day and night sometimes, from a restricted number. She'd answer, and someone would be on the other end, not saying anything," Isabel says. "She stopped answering them after the first few times. But then she said sometimes she'd be somewhere, and she'd get this chill down her spine, like someone was watching her. She'd look around and would never notice anything unusual, but she still couldn't shake that feeling. After a while, she never wanted to be alone anywhere. Any little errand she needed to run, she'd ask me to tag along. Nail salon. Grocery store. Grabbing a quick meal. Running errands."

So that explains why they were so inseparable: Isabel made Celia feel safe. Celia made Isabel feel in love.

"I never said anything to Celia, but I started to wonder if Rob was stepping out behind her back," she says. "My imagination tends to run wild sometimes, but I imagined maybe he had something casual on the side but the side chick wanted more and went psycho when he refused. Which I know sounds like the plot of some made-for-TV movie. But why else would he be so desperate to take that job in Kansas City? He has a good job here. Everyone loves him at the hospital. He's the best administrator they've had in decades."

"How'd you know about the job offer?" I don't recall discussing that with her.

"Everyone talks at the office," she says with an eye roll. "Everyone knew Rob was looking for another job. Everyone but Celia, apparently. And I didn't want to be the one to tell her. I heard Rob had applied at half a dozen other hospitals before getting the offer in Missouri."

"Why would he want to uproot their life here?"

Isabel tosses her hands in the air. "Your guess is as good as mine. But I think it's interesting that her husband was looking for a job and she was being followed and now all of a sudden she's missing. There has to be another woman involved somewhere in this equation."

"You know . . . yesterday I stopped by their house because I hadn't heard from Rob since he went looking for Celia in the city," I say. "And he came to the door with this note in his hand, claiming that I wrote it, and then he went on this crazy-eyed tangent about me being jealous of her. And before he slammed the door in my face, he told me we had to be out of their rental house by the end of the month."

Isabel's mouth forms a circle. "Holy shit."

"I was shaking when I left . . . I've never been spoken to the way he spoke to me, with pure, unadulterated hatred."

"That sounds like a man who's at the end of his rope," she says. "A man whose life is about to implode."

"I mean, in his defense, his wife is missing, and he hadn't slept in days," I say. "But he seemed to be awfully convinced that I wrote this note and secretly wanted to ruin her birthday because I was jealous of her life. The whole thing is just absurd."

"It's got to be Rob," Isabel says. "It's always the husband."

CHAPTER 31

Genevieve

Present day

I stir the simmering pepper pot soup Tuesday night before placing the yeast rolls in the oven.

It feels wrong to be making my husband's favorite meal when my sister is still missing, but the events of the past few days have made me realize how dilapidated my home life has become. My marriage is falling apart at the seams, my daughter is on a direct flight to becoming everything I never wanted her to be, and none of us are happy.

"Smells good," Brad says when he comes in the back door. He's been out in the garage, tinkering with his truck since I got home. We exchanged our usual brief hellos, and not once did he offer to help me carry in the groceries, but I can't expect him to read my mind when I've never required him to in the first place. This marriage isn't going to mend itself, and it's not going to happen overnight. If I have to make the first move, so be it.

"Pepper pot soup." I place the ladle on a spoon rest.

"Really?" His face lights up like a child's at Christmas. Who knew an old soup recipe would be all it took to see an expression I haven't seen in ages?

Brad grabs a spoon from the drawer, lifts the lid on the soup pot, and helps himself to a sample.

"Mm, a guy could get used to this," he moans, wrapping his arm around my waist and pulling me into him. "You're *back*."

"What makes you think I ever left?"

He loosens his grip on me, the look in his eyes suggesting he didn't mean to offend.

"I just meant . . . this takes me back to the early days," he says with a boyish gleam.

I think of our younger selves, practically babies fresh out of high school. The attraction was real. The chemistry was there. But other than that, we had no idea what we were doing. We were a couple of eighteen-year-old virgins playing the part of a husband and his wife. Still, we had fun figuring things out together.

It wasn't always the way it is now.

I used to enjoy throwing on an apron and cooking a meal he'd be talking about for days. And he used to put in forty hours a week and wear his breadwinner hat with a proud twinkle in his eye. Our roles were stereotypes, conventional, and a bit old fashioned, but it worked for us.

We were happy.

We can be happy again.

I *want* to be happy.

I want *him* to be happy, too.

"Where's Charlie?" I ask. "It's too quiet around here."

"She's babysitting," he says. "I also had her put away her laundry before she left."

"And she actually did it?"

"She did."

I turn to face him, leaning against the countertops. For the first time in a long time, I'm actually enjoying my husband's company. If I squint hard enough, I almost see a younger version of him looking back at me. It warms me from the inside out, but only for a moment. It's fleeting, as always. Maybe one day it'll stick around long enough for me to enjoy it.

"Any word on Celia?" he asks.

"No," I say, "but I went to see Isabel today."

"Again?" he asks. I hadn't realized he was paying attention when I filled him in last night.

"She said Celia may have had a stalker," I say. "For the last couple years, she'd been getting strange phone calls and had this feeling like she was being watched."

"Did she ever go to the police about it?"

"I don't think so?"

The timer on the oven chimes. I take out the rolls, and without saying a word, Brad sets the table. I ladle two soup bowls and throw the bread in a paper towel–lined basket. On my way to the table, I pluck a bottle of his favorite IPA from the fridge.

"Thanks, babe," he says, his gaze lingering on me for once instead of passing through me. "You didn't have to do that."

I do, though. I have to do this. *We* have to do this.

That's how this works.

I walk his way, he walks mine, and we meet in the middle. That's where the common ground is. That's where our happiness lies, waiting for us. And if I'm wrong, if there's nothing waiting for us in the middle, then at least we'll have tried.

"So anyway . . ." I continue the conversation because my husband is completely engaged and I'm living for it. Over the hour that follows, I tell Brad *everything*. "So, basically . . . Isabel suspects that Rob was having an affair, that the woman was stalking Celia, and that shit was about to hit the fan, so that's why Rob was so anxious to get out of here. It's just a theory, but still. It makes sense."

Brad takes a swig of his beer, eyes narrowed and distant, like he's digesting the mountain of information I've just heaped onto him over dinner.

"You said that Isabel kissed Celia, right?" he asks.

"Yep."

"And that Isabel is in love with Celia?"

I nod. "That too."

"You also said she took out twenty-five grand for a divorce attorney so she could leave her husband."

"That's what she told me."

"Either she planned on securing some fancy big-time lawyer or she was planning to start a new life somewhere," he says. "What if she made up the stalker thing? What if it's all part of some bigger story they're concocting?"

"You think?" I sit back, contemplating his theory. "Why would she do that? They haven't spoken in months."

"Says who?"

"Says everyone . . . Rob, her hairstylist, *all* of her friends . . ."

Brad takes another drink before pointing the bottle my way. "All I'm saying is, you don't know Isabel that well. Hell, you really don't even know Celia that well. I wouldn't trust either of them as far as I could throw them, especially since Isabel's supposedly in love with Celia and leaving her husband. Maybe Celia was doing the same thing?"

"You have a point. I mean, if Celia was going to leave Rob, this is exactly how she would do it. She'd just . . . be gone."

"Maybe," he says. "Maybe not. You two aren't exactly thick as thieves. There could be a lot you still don't know about her. And as far as Rob goes, screw the bastard. I never did like him anyway. He wants us out? I'll start packing tonight. Just say the word."

"I haven't even started looking for another place . . ." My words fade into nothing, lost with my thoughts. Schofield isn't exactly known for its affordability. I might be able to find us a two-bedroom apartment in the next town over, but that would mean Charlie would have to switch schools again, and I'd hate to do that to her after she's already settled in here and found her place with a nice group of friends. "I'm hoping once he realizes it wasn't me who wrote that note, he'll calm down. Maybe give us more time. He can't expect us to find something in less than two weeks."

"Whatever happens, we'll land on our feet," he says. "I'll make sure of that."

His words are a balm to my soul, but they're meaningless without effort behind them.

Still, I want to believe this is his way of meeting me in the middle.

"You know, they're hiring again in tech support at Eastward," I say. "There's a thousand-dollar sign-on bonus and another thousand-dollar referral bonus if you stay on at least six months."

Brad rises from the table, working his way to my side. He places his hand on my shoulder, bends down, and kisses the top of my head.

"I'll do you one better than that," he says.

In the earliest years of our marriage, I stayed home while Brad got a degree from Cross Beach College in entrepreneurship. Turns out it's a useless degree unless you're a silver-spooned kid with parents willing to funnel seed money into your business ideas. With his father being a church pastor and his mother staying home full time, there wasn't much money for seeding, and eventually Brad traded his ambitions for a stable paycheck.

In the end, he took various odd jobs. For a few years he sold used cars. After that, he worked in the office at a local college as a recruiter. He spent time as a carpenter one summer, and the following year, he tried his hand at an HVAC apprenticeship. Nothing Brad has done has ever fulfilled him or sustained us.

"And what's that?" I ask.

"I got on at the utility company in town," he says. "Starting pay is twenty-two fifty an hour plus overtime. I report the first of next month. They'll train me for the first thirty days, then I'll shadow some guys for the next sixty; after that I'll be on my own."

"Brad, that's wonderful." I rise and throw my arms around his shoulders, breathing in his diesel-and-concrete scent. The man loves to work with his hands and spend as much time outside as possible. If we're lucky, this one might stick. "This is great news."

But a celebration feels out of place in this moment, considering all that's going on.

Brad's eyes hold on mine, lingering, as if he can sense the heaviness weighing me down.

"Why don't you go lie down a bit," he says. "I'll do the dishes."

"I won't argue with that."

I resist the urge to tell him which GladWare container to use for the leftover soup, and I bite my tongue instead of reminding him which pots and pans need to be hand-washed and which ones are dishwasher safe.

Instead, I head to the hall bathroom, run myself the hottest bath I can stand, and soak the day away, replaying Isabel's theories about Rob against Brad's theories about Isabel. I may not know the truth yet, but I do know this: one of them clearly has something to hide.

CHAPTER 32

Genevieve

Present day

"You've got to be kidding me," Rob says Wednesday when he opens his front door. I'm on my lunch break, and I don't have much time. I'd have called and given him a heads-up, but I'm positive he would've ignored me.

I cut to the chase. "Did you know Celia had a stalker?"

His face is pinched. "What? No. What are you talking about?"

"One of her friends"—I don't tell him whom—"says she'd been dealing with harassing phone calls and thought she was being followed."

"Don't you think I'd know if my wife was being harassed?" he asks. "Celia never said a word about any of that stuff. And who told you that?"

"I'd rather not say."

"You'd rather not say because you're pulling it out of your ass," he says with authoritative confidence. "I can assure you, my wife was not being stalked. Who would even stalk her? The only person I can think of who'd be crazy enough to do something like that is Isabel Delvy, and she didn't need to stalk Celia because the two of them were together twenty-four seven."

I don't tell him it's because Celia was afraid to be alone.

"There's a rumor," I say carefully, though I'm taking liberties with the definition of "rumor." It's more of a theory than anything. And I want to test him. I want to gauge his reaction. "But some people claim you were having an affair and that your mistress was the one stalking Celia, and that's the reason you wanted to leave Schofield."

His face turns the color of pickled beets again, and his lips are tight against his teeth.

"I have *never*, and I would *never*, cheat on my wife," he says, pointing his finger mere inches from my face.

"Then why suddenly feel the urge to uproot your entire life?"

"It wasn't a sudden urge, not that it's any of your business. I've worked at Schofield General for fifteen years now. The bureaucracy was getting to be too much. Not to mention I was bored. I wanted a change, and quite frankly, Genevieve, I don't owe you an explanation."

"I'm sure you can see how the timing of all of this is interesting."

"Stop with the lies, Genevieve. Stop inventing theories. Stop making this ten times worse than it already is. I'm warning you."

"Lies?" I ignore his warning. "I'm trying to find the truth."

"You're not trying to find the truth; you're trying to take the heat off yourself." Conviction runs rampant in his tone. "You wrote that note. You're the only one who would've done something petty and childish like that. You're the reason she left. You're the reason she hasn't been herself the last two years. You're a miserable wench, and you'll stop at nothing to bring everyone down to your level. You can't stand to see anyone else happy because it reminds you of your own unhappiness. Well, guess what? This world doesn't owe you a damn thing, and neither does your sister. You should've been happy for her all these years, for getting away from your psychotic parents. Instead you hated her for doing all the things you were too scared to do."

My breath is shallow as I swallow all the terrible things I want to scream in his face.

He couldn't be more wrong.

"You know, I thought it was strange how you went from not giving a damn about Celia for twenty years to suddenly spending every spare second you have trying to find her. If that doesn't scream guilt, I don't know what does." A sneer claims his thin mouth.

"I *always* gave a damn about my sister," I say, my expression as steely and unforgiving as a prison's barbed wire fence. "And I still do."

I leave before he gets a reaction out of me.

He doesn't deserve the satisfaction.

CHAPTER 33

GENEVIEVE

Present day

"They finally ran a piece about Celia," Brad says when I get home Wednesday night. He points the remote at the TV, rewinds the five-o'clock news, and cues up a segment that begins with a cropped image of a cheerful, relaxed, suntanned Celia. I recognize it from her fireplace mantel—it's one of her and Rob standing on a beach. "About damn time."

"New at five . . . The police are asking for the public's help in locating missing Schofield resident Celia Guest," a strawberry blonde news anchor says. "The forty-year-old woman was last seen by friends Friday evening at the French Salt Bar on Millington Avenue in downtown Schofield. Police say she and her husband went home, and she left the premises sometime around three in the morning. Investigators believe she drove to the Metro-North train station and purchased a ticket to Grand Central. Security footage shows her climbing aboard the five twenty-two train. Her whereabouts are still unknown. If you've seen Celia or have any information, please call the number on your screen."

Brad pauses the TV, my sister's haunting image frozen on the screen.

"It's been almost five days," I say, dropping my purse on the ground and kicking off my shoes. "Five days and they're just *now* taking it seriously?"

"It's bullshit," he says.

"They should've done this days ago—they should've done this the morning she was gone. What if someone saw something over the weekend? What if they could've spoken up sooner? What if she could be home by now?"

Brad rises from his recliner, making his way to me. Pressing his hands into my tense shoulder muscles, he kneads the tender knots. But my muscles remain stiff. I couldn't possibly relax.

"I'm so sorry, Gen," he says after a silent beat.

Is he sorry? Or is he simply saying the words he thinks I need to hear? He's never been crazy about my sister. He's always kept his comments to himself, but a woman knows the look of disgust in her husband's eyes when she sees it. He never needed to say how he felt—it was written on his face every time they were in the room together.

To be fair, I'm certain the feeling goes both ways.

"You know, the longer someone's gone, the less likely they are to come home." My voice is broken, each word burning the back of my throat. "I looked it up today, the statistics."

"Don't think like that. You can't. It's not over until it's over."

"What if it's never over?" I turn to him, my voice breaking in my tightened throat. "What if she just . . . stays gone forever?"

The thought of never seeing my sister again, never having the chance to truly get to know her, places an unbearable weight on my chest.

"I don't know, Gen. I don't have the answers you're looking for," he says. "Wish I did."

Without another word, he pulls me into his arms. For the first time in a long time, I let him hold me. I welcome comfort from another human being, as strange as it feels, because while it's a foreign sensation, it feels like home at the same time.

A lifetime ago, Celia felt like home, too.

I let my husband hold me awhile longer before I head to our room, peel out of my work clothes, and shuffle to the kitchen to start dinner.

I'm preheating the oven when my phone rings—and Rob's name flashes on the screen.

"Hello?" I answer.

"They found her, Gen," he says, his tone laced with enough excitement to cause a flutter of hope to dance through my center. "They found Celia."

I brace myself on the counter ledge to keep from falling to the floor.

"Who found her?" I ask, my lips wavy and numb. A million other questions rattle through my head, all demanding to be next. "Where is she? Is she okay? Where has she been? What was she doing?"

The room tilts, so I take a seat on the closest barstool.

"She's in Manhattan—NewYork-Presbyterian Hospital. I'm on my way there right now."

"Can you pick me up on the way?" I'll act like we didn't bite each other's heads off earlier if he will—I just need to see her.

"Be there in ten," he says without hesitation, a confirmation that everything before is now water under the bridge.

"What was that about?" Brad appears in the doorway, scratching his temple and watching me maneuver around the room in a daze.

"They found her. They found Celia."

CHAPTER 34

GENEVIEVE

Ten years ago

"You want me to put her to bed tonight?" Brad asks when he carries our sleeping daughter in from the car. We went to my parents' tonight for dinner, an unofficial celebration for Celeste's sixteenth birthday. When she wasn't looking, I slipped her a Starbucks gift card. We've come a long way from tea roses and shiny rocks.

"Yeah, if you don't mind?" I massage my temples. "I've got a bit of a headache. Must be that storm front coming in. Going to take something and soak in the tub for a bit."

Brad leans in to steal a kiss, and I linger to watch him haul Charlie to her room. I love how tiny she looks in his arms and how delicate he is with her. He's a good dad. More hands-on than the one I had, that's for sure. And he lets us celebrate her birthday the proper way—with a cake and candles and presents. It's always just the three of us, of course. His parents, like mine, have never believed in that sort of "self-centered nonsense."

It turns out Brad's upbringing as the pastor's kid wasn't much different from mine.

We spent the majority of our initial courtship dissecting our parents' marriages and making pacts and pledges to one another that ours would be different—better.

So far, so good.

We both work outside the home. Charlie goes to a public day care. We attend church once a week—no more, no less. We've never inflicted any sort of physical punishments on our daughter—and we never will.

I chase two Advil with a glass of tap water before locking myself in the cramped bathroom of our two-bedroom apartment. We're saving up for a house, but until then, we're cozy and comfortable here.

Ten minutes later, I'm basting in a steamy, hot tub, scrolling mindlessly on my phone while I wait for the throbbing in my head to subside.

It's hard to believe Celeste is sixteen now, but it's even harder to imagine Celia at thirty. In my mind's eye, she's still eighteen and still very much sporting her baby face.

Biting my lip, I tap on my phone's internet browser.

Every time I do this, I wind up more disappointed than the time before. Yet I've never given up hope that one of these days I might actually find her.

I type "Celia Fielding" into the search bar, hold my breath, and press enter.

Half a second later, I'm presented with the same 3.3 million results as the last time, and I comb through the first dozen or so pages hoping to find a thread begging to be unraveled. But there isn't anyone on here who could remotely be my sister.

I run another search, this time inquiring about legal documents. Maybe there's a chance she changed her name or got married?

The top result promises unlimited search privileges for courts in all fifty states for a mere $89.99. It takes a minute or two of hovering my thumb over the buy button before I finally bite the bullet. Brad would be upset with me for wasting perfectly good grocery money on something like this, but I have to know.

An hour later, my bathwater is barely lukewarm—but I stumbled upon a record for a marriage license in Connecticut between a Celia Fielding and a Robert Guest. Sitting up, I all but choke on my spit when I recall the summer Celia worked for Guest Accounting Services—and ran off with the owner's son, never to be heard from again.

It has to be her.

I run a search on "Celia Guest" and sift through a bunch of misses before finally getting a hit in the form of an article about her husband, Robert, being named the new administrator for a hospital in Schofield, Connecticut. The write-up goes on for a solid paragraph about Robert's background in nursing home and medical clinic administration as well as his two graduate degrees. The final line mentions his wife: "Robert lives in Schofield with his wife, Celia."

Connecticut?

It seems . . . random . . . but if this is her—and I believe that it is—at least she's alive.

Dampness blurs my vision, but I'm consumed with so many sensations at once that I'm not sure if my tears are happy or sad or some strange combination of the two.

Collecting myself, I wipe the tears away and search for her on all my social media accounts. My efforts turn up nothing, though I'm not surprised.

She isn't hiding . . . She just doesn't want to be found.

My mind fills with question after question, curiosities nagging my every thought.

Does she ever think about me? About Celeste? Does she miss us? Does she ever think about reaching out? Does she have regrets?

Growing up, I often heard stories about deadbeat moms or dads who abandoned their families, but there were never any about kids getting abandoned by their older siblings. I had no one to talk to and no way to process my feelings about any of it. My parents refused to say her name—she was dead to them. And Celeste was too young to remember her and too busy being the apple of my parents' eyes.

A shiver runs through me, and I place my phone aside before draining the cold bathwater.

Maybe I should be happy for my sister, that she got out from under our oppressive upbringing, that she met someone and fell in love. But now that I know she's alive and well and hasn't made a single attempt to reach out, there isn't an ounce of happiness flooding my veins.

Instead, my whole being feels heavy, and my thoughts grow dark.

CHAPTER 35

GENEVIEVE

Present day

I don't recognize the woman lying in the hospital bed, connected to wires and machines. A portion of her beautiful auburn hair is shaved clean to the scalp, nothing but a meandering incision peppered with staples to hold it shut. It isn't until I take a step closer and inspect her swollen face for the signature freckle above her left eyebrow that I accept the fact that the battered and blue woman lying before me is none other than my sister.

"Celia." I slide my hand into hers. There's a burn in the back of my throat, as if words are trying to make their way out, but I haven't got a clue what to say.

Rob hasn't uttered a word since we walked in here. He hasn't taken his eyes off her for one second either. He simply walked in, pulled a chair up to her bed, and placed his hand on hers.

On the drive to the train station a couple of hours ago, Rob put Detective Samuels on speakerphone so he could fill us in.

So far the police have pieced together a handful of details: Celia was staying at a hotel in an unfamiliar-to-her neighborhood, went out for a walk Saturday night, then got mugged and assaulted on the way home.

The person who attacked her stole her phone and wallet—at least that's what they assume because they could find neither of those things in her possession when they found her. Miraculously, she made it back to her room after the brutal assault, where she must have lain down on the bed—and passed out.

The doctor I spoke with outside her room a moment ago said it isn't out of the realm of possibility that this happened the way they imagine it did. He said she was probably in a fight-or-flight stage and so fueled by adrenaline, she didn't realize how bad of shape she was in. He said if a person has enough adrenaline coursing through them, it works to distract them from the pain—a built-in survival mechanism of sorts. He then added it's not unusual for someone with a head injury as severe as hers to fall asleep . . . and not wake up.

The night after her attack, the hotel clerk realized Celia hadn't checked out and hadn't paid for another night. She sent the maintenance man to check on her. That's when she was discovered unresponsive on the bed.

They called 9-1-1 immediately, though they were unable to provide any name or information since she paid with cash and her ID and phone were gone. The doctor said if they hadn't called for help when they did, there's a chance Celia might not have survived.

With her face swollen beyond recognition, it was nearly impossible for them to determine her identity. It wasn't until she woke up for the first time today and managed to give them her name that the nurse ran a Google search and discovered she was missing out of Schofield.

"I'm so sorry." Celia's eyes remain closed, but her words are crystal clear.

I hadn't realized she was awake.

"Celia, don't." Rob pats her hand. "Don't apologize. Just rest."

I study him for something—a hint or a sign that he's silencing her rather than comforting her—but his expression is unreadable.

I get nothing.

CHAPTER 36

GENEVIEVE

Three years ago

I hold my phone with trembling hands. With Celia's phone number queued up and my thumb hovering over the call button, I draw in a long, slow breath. I found her information behind a paywall of some white pages website, and I paid fifty bucks to see it without knowing if it was current or even correct.

I tap the green circle and bring the phone to my ear. It rings right away. Once. Twice. Three times. I'm mentally preparing my voice mail when a woman's voice comes on the line.

"Hello?"

"H-hi," I say. "Is this Celia Guest?"

She's quiet for a beat.

"Yes," she finally says. "Who's calling?"

"Is this Celia . . . *Fielding* . . . Guest?" I ask.

"Who is this?"

I swallow the impossibly hard lump in my throat. "It's Genevieve."

Bracing myself, I fully expect her to hang up, and after a few moments of silence, I peel the phone from my ear and check to see if she's still there.

She is.

"I'm calling because . . . Mom died," I say. "Um, yesterday. She had cancer."

I debate whether to give her the full rundown, and then I decide against it. It doesn't matter. It won't change anything.

"I just thought you should know," I add. The silence between us is excruciating. I can't even get a read on whether she's upset about my having her number. "I won't bother you again, I just—"

She cuts me off. "I'm very sorry for your loss." Only her words aren't cold; they're warm and genuine. "That must be so difficult for you."

I'm taken aback for a second, but I gather myself. "Thank you. We, um, we had time to prepare. It wasn't unexpected. She was in hospice in the end . . ."

Again, I'm not sure how much she cares to know.

"Anyway, the wake is in two days, and the funeral is the day after that," I say. "It's here in Cross Beach, at the church."

"I won't be attending, but thank you."

"I didn't expect you to," I say.

More silence settles between us, almost as if neither of us is ready to hang up yet, though for reasons of our own.

"It's good to hear your voice," she says, her words slightly fragmented, like a person trying to smile through tears. "I've thought of you often over the years, but I was afraid to reach out. I figured you must hate me for leaving the way I did . . . Are you doing okay? Are you happy? Are you healthy? Tell me everything."

The hardness around my heart turns soft and pliable, and I sink into my living room sofa. The protective armor around my emotions fades away. All the hard-edged animosity I've harbored toward her fades into background noise.

I don't know where to begin; I just know that this is a conversation I've been waiting to have for nearly two decades. Now that it's happening, I can hardly form the words.

"You still there?" she asks.

"Yes," I manage. "I'm still here."

Over the two hours that follow, I tell my sister everything. I tell her what it was like after she left. I tell her about Celeste. I tell her about my courtship and eventual marriage to Pastor Jacobs's son. And then I tell her about Charlie, which inevitably segues into our battle with infertility, which then leads into Brad's constant job-hopping, which then brings us to our current bankruptcy and impending foreclosure. By the time I'm finished, I'm nothing but snot and tears, yet at the same time there's a lightness in my chest that hasn't been there in ages.

I grab a Kleenex from the box beside me and wipe the mess from my face.

"I'm so sorry," I say with a nervous chuckle. "You probably weren't expecting all of that."

"Don't be sorry at all," Celia says. "Maybe next time you can give me the unabridged version?"

Next time?

All I wanted was a minute of her time today to share the news about Mom . . . and now she's talking about there being a next time?

The rumble of Brad's truck steals my elation before I get a chance to respond. He's home with Charlie. This conversation's over.

"Are you sure you don't want to come to the funeral?" I ask.

"I'm sure. And even if I wanted to, Dad would never allow that."

I worry the inside of my lip, watching my husband and daughter make their way up the front walk.

"Can I see you sometime?" I ask.

"You feel like taking a trip up here?" she asks with a half laugh, almost as if she expects me to say no. "My treat. I feel like I owe you at least that."

"Sure," I say as the front door swings open. Brad and Charlie kick off their shoes. He hasn't shown an ounce of emotion since my mother passed—not that I expected him to. Charlie, on the other hand, has been crying off and on. She was Mom's only grandchild, and the two of them had quite a bond, though I've often wondered if she was vying to replace Brad's mom as the favorite grandmother.

My mother was a lot of things . . . complicated, perfectionistic, high strung. But most of all, she was quietly competitive.

"I'll start looking at flights," Celia says. "How soon could you come?"

I feel like I've been waiting my whole life to hear her say those words.

CHAPTER 37

Genevieve

Present day

I bump into Rob by the vending machines Friday afternoon. I managed to take a half day from work so I could spend more time with Celia, and I brought a weekend bag as well, fully prepared to sleep on a cot, pullout couch, waiting room chair—anything.

I'm not leaving her side any longer than I have to.

Rob hasn't left the hospital once. Whether that's endearing or suspicious has yet to be determined.

"Hey," I say.

Ever since he called me two nights ago and said they found Celia, we haven't said more than a handful of words to one another. After the call with the detective, the rest of the ride was silence and road noise.

At the train station, we bought our tickets together but sat in opposite aisles. Maybe he feels sheepish about going off on me earlier in the week and accusing me of wanting to sabotage my sister's happiness?

But now here we are, standing in front of a humming Pepsi machine, pretending like nothing happened.

He clears his throat, staring straight ahead at the brightly lit appliance. "Hi."

"How's she doing?" I ask. "I just got here . . ."

"Better."

"Just better? Have they said when she can go home? Has she said much about what led up to anything?"

"We have to take this one day at a time. Right now, she's lucky to be alive," he says. "Let's just focus on that."

I swipe my debit card, grab a diet cherry Pepsi, and head down the hall to her room. I'll be lucky if I get thirty seconds alone with her before he waltzes in like a valiant prince on his noble steed.

"Hey there." I find her awake, her swollen, bloodshot eyes fixed on the muted TV mounted in the corner. It's tuned to some afternoon soap opera, and judging by the intensity in the actors' eyes, someone's about to get slapped or poisoned.

She blinks a couple of times before realizing who I am.

"Sorry," she says, her voice still froggy. "My vision's still a little blurry. Thought you were the nurse for a second. I'm about due for my next round of pain pills."

I take the seat that's already nudged against her bed, likely where Rob's been planted all day.

"How are you feeling?" I ask.

"Like I got hit by a Mack truck and a freight train at the same time."

The doctors told us the other day that she had a parietal fracture, severe concussion, and an acute subdural hematoma—the last of which likely caused her unconsciousness and is also highly fatal in almost half of all cases. The last of which also required an emergency craniotomy to remove the pressure from her brain.

We're told it could take weeks, months, or even years for her to make a complete recovery, and even then she may not be 100 percent.

In the meantime, headaches, nausea, blurred vision, and mood swings are to be expected.

"I just want to go home," she says.

The question lingers on the tip of my tongue, begging to be spoken into existence, but it's not the time or place. And with Rob about to walk in here any moment, I don't want to risk it on the off chance he's the reason she left in the first place.

"The doctors said it might be another week or so," I remind her in case she forgot.

I glance at the doorway, waiting, watching, tempted to ask.

"Rob says you were on a mission to find me," Celia says. Her lips inch into a smile that quickly becomes a pained wince.

I'm grateful he's giving credit where credit's due, but I imagine he didn't mention I accused him of having an affair or that he accused me of ruining her birthday with a cruel and cryptic note.

"We were worried, Celia," I say. "We all were. A lot of people care about you."

I called Celeste last night to give her an update, and she was more excited than I expected. I don't share that with Celia. Not yet.

"It's the strangest thing, Gen. I just went out for some air . . ." Her eyelids drift shut. "And now I'm here."

I steal another peek toward the doorway, confirming Rob is still out of sight before I inch closer.

"Do you remember what happened?" I ask. "Do you remember anything?"

She swallows, her lips pale and dry. "Not really. Bits and pieces, nothing concrete. My recollection is . . . elusive. It's like trying to remember a dream."

I'm not surprised. The doctors said short-term memory loss was common with traumatic brain injuries.

"Were you running away from something?" I keep my voice low. "Or someone?"

She opens her eyes, her bruised gaze searching mine until the sound of sneakers against tile floor steals the moment out from under us.

"Celia, you're awake," Rob says, a Styrofoam coffee cup in hand as he joins us.

He places a spare chair next to mine, takes a seat, and doesn't leave her side until visiting hours are over.

It occurs to me on the journey home the next morning that maybe he still believes I had something to do with that note . . . that perhaps he thinks *he's* protecting *her* from *me*. That or he's worried I might mention the alleged affair.

Either way, he doesn't want me alone with her.

And either way, I'm going to keep digging until I strike the cold, hard truth.

It's in there somewhere, buried deep, waiting to see the light of day. With any luck, that day will be soon.

CHAPTER 38

CELIA

Present day

"Who was it?" I ask my sister when she returns from answering the door. I've been home a handful of days . . . I think. Time tends to blur together now. Rob tells me the incident happened two weeks ago, but sometimes it feels like it never happened at all. If it weren't for the massive headaches that come on without warning, the double vision, and my shoddy memory, I'd be in better shape. I suppose it's a blessing that I don't remember what happened that night in the city.

"Another reporter," Genevieve says with an irritated sigh. "I wish Rob would just give them a statement so they'd quit showing up like this."

"The police have asked him not to," I say. "But I get it. People are worried, that's all."

"You're recovering from a traumatic brain injury. The least they can do is not knock on the door in the middle of the day without calling."

The shower is still running in the en suite. Since I've been home, Rob rarely leaves my side. He's always been protective of me, but now the intensity has been ratcheted up a few notches.

"Are you hungry? I brought some soup from your favorite deli," Genevieve says. "Or I can make you something? Rob just had groceries delivered this morning."

The medications I'm on have dulled my appetite—an ironic side effect given I'm supposed to eat when I take them.

I'm about to take her up on her offer when the doorbell rings . . . again.

"Ugh." Genevieve disappears into the next room, her footsteps growing distant.

A minute later, she returns with an oversized bouquet of pristine white roses accented with baby's breath. Ever since I've been home, Rob and Gen have been fielding deliveries and phone calls from friends and well-wishers. Neal and Deanna dropped off a meal the first night. Deirdre and Holly sent me a video message telling me they missed me and wished me a speedy recovery. Natalie stopped by the second night for a quick visit, followed by Margaux. The next-door neighbors sent a flower arrangement from their garden, while Clint and Adam have been texting Rob for updates, not wanting to bother me during my recovery. But this bouquet is ridiculously oversized, comically so. And white—an interesting choice of color, one normally reserved for occasions marked by purity and innocence. First communions. Weddings. The birth of a baby.

"That is massive," I say as Genevieve carefully places it on my dresser. Judging from the amount of space it takes up, it has to span at least two feet wide. "Can you open the card for me? I have no idea who would've sent me something like this."

"It's probably one of those cable news networks trying to get an exclusive interview with—" She stops speaking when she reads the card, and then her brows lift.

"What?" I ask.

"It's just . . . not what I expected." She makes her way to my side of the bed and hands me the card, her eyes holding an unspoken apology.

CELIA—

WISHES FOR A SPEEDY RECOVERY . . . GOD KNOWS YOU DESERVE IT.

YOUR SISTER,

CELESTE

"I hope you're not upset, but I was keeping Celeste updated over the past week," Genevieve says. "I had no idea she was going to send you flowers."

The room tilts, and the sting of hot bile rises from the back of my throat.

"Oh, my God. Are you okay? You're white as a sheet." Genevieve takes the card from my hand, places it on my nightstand, and exchanges it for my glass of water. "Here, drink this. I'm going to grab your meds. I'll be right back."

She trots off, and I take a sip. The cold water does nothing to appease the heat creeping through every part of me or the nauseating swell in my middle.

My sister returns with a couple of pill bottles.

"Did you give her my address?" I ask as the prickle of anxious sweat beads along the back of my neck.

Genevieve taps one pill from each container into her palm before handing them to me.

Her brows meet. "I did . . . Is that a problem?"

I don't know how to answer her honestly without prompting a conversation I've spent the better part of my life avoiding.

I toss the pills back, but they get stuck in my dry throat. It takes three generous gulps to wash them down.

"They're just *flowers*, Celia . . ." she says, probably sensing the tension in the room. "From your *sister* . . . It's very thoughtful of her, don't you think?"

She stops to admire the arrangement, adjusting stems and greenery until they suit her liking.

"You know, she'd love to get to know you," Genevieve says. Turning toward me, she gathers a soft breath. "When you're ready, of course."

"If you don't mind, I feel like resting for a bit," I say, changing the subject before we have a chance to get too deep into it.

"Of course." She waves her hand, trekking backward to the door. "I'll just be out here if you need me."

The sound of the shower spray dies out. A few minutes later, Rob steps out of the en suite, his hair wet and the scent of his aftershave emanating from his direction.

His face fills with a charming smile, the way it always does when he sees me, no matter how long we've been apart.

His smile disappears the instant he notices something's off.

"What's wrong?" He makes his way to my side of the bed.

"Just feeling a little nauseated." I fan my face. "Think I'm going to try and get a nap in; hopefully it'll be gone when I wake up."

"Must be the meds. All those nasty side effects must be taking a toll on you." Rob adjusts my covers, pulls the blinds closed on the window, and gifts me a tender kiss before leaving me to rest.

I should have had him take the roses on his way.

I don't need a reminder of what happened that day.

I already think about it all the time.

CHAPTER 39

CELIA

Twenty-six years ago

"Celia, wake up." A whispering voice in my ear is followed by the gentle shake of my mattress. "Be quiet now. Don't wake your sister or your mother."

"What's going on?" I whisper back to him. The clock on my nightstand reads 12:01 AM.

I'm officially fourteen years old—is this some kind of birthday surprise? When I was eight, my parents woke my sister and me up at six one morning. We piled in the car and drove three hours until we got to Orlando. They surprised us with a trip to Disney World for no reason at all. It was our first—and last—time ever doing such a thing, but I swear I could close my eyes and remember every last detail about that day. The smell of coffee and gas station doughnuts in the car, watching the sun come up as we drove down a stretch of coastal highway, the crowd of people in line, all shoulder to shoulder, smelling like deodorant and sunscreen.

"Get your shoes on." He doesn't answer me. He simply places a pair of sneakers on the floor beside my bed. "Come on now, move a little faster than that, Celia."

Butterflies tickle my stomach as I jam my feet into my sneakers and tie the laces as fast as my little fingers will allow.

He motions for me to follow him to the hall and then out the back door, where his car is idling by the garage. I don't think I've ever stayed up past midnight in my life. The world's a little quieter now, the stars a little brighter. It's as eerie as it is magical.

I climb in the back seat, where I always sit, and he shifts into reverse.

"Where are we going?" I ask again.

His knuckles are white against the steering wheel. "You'll see when we get there."

For the next ten minutes, I stare out the window, bleary eyed, watching the sleeping world go by. I think about this day fourteen years ago, when my parents welcomed me into the world. My mother says her water broke in the middle of the night when my dad was on patrol. It took him a while to get home, and by the time he got her to the hospital, she was fully dilated and ready to push. The story ends with my father passing out the second they placed me on my mother. He's always had a weak stomach when it comes to childbirth or anything surrounding the female condition.

He slows to a stop outside a small blue house with boarded windows. The other houses on the street are blacked out, no lights inside, no cars in the drive. I've never been to this side of town before, but I've heard my father talk about it from time to time when it involves work matters. Squatters, mostly, or kids sneaking out here to do drugs or vandalize anything that hasn't already been vandalized.

Without a word, he climbs out of the car and unlatches the trunk. By the time I follow, his arms are loaded with towels, bottled water, blankets, and what appears to be a medical textbook.

My excitement has vanished, replaced with sheer confusion and a heavy, sinking sensation in the bottom of my stomach.

"Come on, Celia, we don't have time to waste." He jogs toward the front door, prying it open.

The house smells of rotted wood and mildew. It takes a minute for my eyes to adjust, but when they do, I'm met with the remains of a long since abandoned living room. A plaid sofa with slashed cushions. A broken recliner. A wooden coffee table littered with ashtrays and needles.

A strange sound comes from the hallway, some kind of moaning—like someone's hurt.

"This way." My father motions for me to follow him.

The sounds grow louder with each step, almost drowned out by the oceanic whoosh of my heartbeat in my ears.

When we reach the bedroom at the end of the hall, he nudges the door open with an elbow and steps aside. In the dark, I make out a female figure lying on a bed, her legs spread wide and tears streaming down her cheeks.

"It's all right now," my father says to the woman. "Celia's here now. She's going to get us through this."

He crouches to the side of the bed, taking her hand in his.

It's then that I see the swollen belly.

A wash of shock runs through me, only to be overrun by a second wave when I realize who the woman on the bed is: Alison Lang—our babysitter.

"Come on, Celia." My father grabs the medical textbook, flipping it to a dog-eared page in the middle. "I need you to deliver this baby."

"I . . . I don't . . . I can't . . ." I stammer and stutter. I don't know the first thing about delivering babies.

"You're going to have to learn really quick, sweetheart." His tone is laced in sarcasm with a side of desperation as Alison squeezes his hand and screams out in pain, mumbling something about it burning.

I clench my thighs in sympathy.

I saw a movie once where the female character gave birth. She was sweaty and screaming and yelling—much like Alison now—but it seemed like the entire thing only took three or four minutes.

Time stands still around this moment, yet everything's happening so fast.

By the time Alison says, "I feel like I need to push," I'm not sure if we've been here five minutes or five hours. I reckon it's somewhere in between.

"Celia, I need you to catch the baby when it comes out," my father says. "I'm going to grab something from my car, I'll be right back."

In the dark, dank room of an abandoned house in a terrifying part of town, I come face-to-face with the girl who used to take us swimming and roller-skating, who used to watch Disney movies with us and pretend to paint our toenails with the brush from our watercolor paint set. Even though she's not quite four years older than me, I always wished she could've been my mom. She'd have been a lot more fun than the one I have, that's for sure. All things considered, this baby is lucky to have her.

"Alison." Her name leaves my lips in a hollow puff of terrified air. "I don't know if I can do this."

"I'm so sorry, Celia, I am. I'm so sorry you have to see me like this." Tears streak down her face. Sweat, maybe. It's hard to tell.

I can't bring myself to look between her legs.

It feels wrong.

She winces, baring her teeth and reaching for a fistful of blanket to clench.

I offer her my hand.

"I don't understand," I manage to say. "Why didn't you go to the hospital? Why are you here?"

The last time Alison babysat for us had to have been around Christmastime. She didn't have a boyfriend then, only a handful of crushes. One boy she spoke about often, though she'd never tell us his name. The only hint she'd give us was that he went to our church.

"Did someone from church do this to you?" I ask. "That boy you liked?"

Alison groans through another contraption . . . *contraction* . . . whatever they're called. I page through the textbook, holding it close to the window so I can read the tiny words with the help of the moonlight pouring in.

"How long am I supposed to push for?" she asks through her teeth.

"I don't know, I don't know . . ." I page through the book, my eyes scanning the words as fast as they'll let me.

My father returns with a small medical kit, laying out gauze and a pair of scissors and a few items I don't recognize.

"When this baby comes out, Celia, you're going to have to clamp the cord in two places once it stops pulsing, and then you're going to cut it with these scissors," he tells me.

"I don't understand why you need my help—you already know what to do." Ordinarily I wouldn't talk back to him like this, but there's nothing ordinary about this situation.

"You know I have a weak stomach for this kind of thing," he says.

"Why can't she go to the hospital?" I ask.

"It's not an option," he says, his voice low despite it being just the three of us. "Her parents don't know she's with child. Neither does the church. She's in a bad place, Celia, and we're going to help her. That's what we do for one another in times like these, and that's what we're doing for this young woman."

She hardly looks like a woman. More like a teenage girl. In this light, practically a child.

A frightened child.

I think of her parents in this moment. Mr. Lang owns the medical equipment company in town, and her mom is a kindergarten teacher. They're good, kind, everyday people. I'd like to think they wouldn't put her out on the street for something like this, but if there's anything I've learned over the years, it's that grown-ups wear personalities like masks, switching them out when the moment calls for it.

My father has his church mask, his police mask, and the mask he wears at home. Probably half a dozen others that I can't think of right now because Alison's screams are reaching a fever pitch.

She cries through another contraction, and my father rushes to her side, giving her his arm to squeeze as he whispers something in her ear and brushes the sticky, sweaty hair from her forehead, the way you'd comfort a person you cared about.

Or loved.

I've never even seen him touch my mother that way, so tender and comforting.

She nuzzles into him, her eyes squeezing tight as she attempts to catch her breath between pushes.

I'm not sure how much time passes between the realization that my father and Alison are acting weird and the agonizing shriek that accompanies a head of dark hair emerging from between her legs. All I know is there were three people in this abandoned house when we got here . . . and now there are four.

My father leaves the room while I wrap the baby in a towel and place her on Alison's chest. She's sticky and warm and pink, and a gurgled cry escapes her lungs. I grab the clamps, place them on the umbilical cord, and wait for the pulsing to stop before making the cut.

Just when I think we're done, the book says something about delivering a placenta.

While Alison coos sweet nothings at her baby, I fight the overwhelming urge to throw up, barely making it outside the door before losing the contents of my stomach on the matted hallway carpet.

"Everything okay?" My father's voice cuts through the dark.

He must have been waiting in the living room.

I catch my breath, nodding, swallowing the acidic remnants in the back of my throat.

"You can go in," I say. But I stop him before he does. "Dad?"

"Yes?"

"Why were you . . . why were you touching Alison like that?" I wipe my mouth on the back of my hand.

He squints, examining me. "Like what?"

I don't know how to describe it; all I know is it made me uncomfortable when I saw it. Looking back, it happened so fast—maybe I imagined it?

"Is that my sister in there?" I straighten my shoulders and brace myself for a smack across the face . . . that never comes.

His lips press into a firm line, and his eyes turn downward. If this is what shame looks like on Jim Fielding, it's the first time I've seen it.

"Don't lie to me, Dad," I say, leaving out a reminder that God is watching, because I'm certain he already knows. He tells us so every day.

My father doesn't answer, but his eyes say it all.

"Why?" I fight back the tears that blind my vision. I'm not sure why I'm so emotional—I'm not the one who cheated. I'm not the one who had a child with a teenage babysitter. I'm not the one who's been living a lie.

"Some things are too complicated to explain to a young lady your age," he says before pushing past me and attending to his newest child.

"Except for childbirth," I say under my breath. He doesn't hear me. He's focused on Alison and their love child.

If my mother knew about this, she'd be devastated. Being his wife is the only thing in this world she lives for—second only to her lord and savior. Gen and I come in last—after the church. If she knew her husband had fallen into sin with someone else . . . someone she knows and trusts . . .

I return to the scene of the birth, but only because this house gives me the creeps and I don't want to be alone in any of these rooms.

"Celia, why don't you help Alison get cleaned up," he says. "We'll put her on the mattress in the next room. I laid some clean bedding down for her."

He hands me an orange-brown prescription bottle with my mother's name on it. The directions on the label say to take one to two pills every four to six hours for pain, as needed. Judging by the date on the label, these are left over from her dental surgery last year.

"Give her four of those," he says.

"But the bottle says—"

He cuts me off and gives me a wild-eyed look, one that dares me to question him. "I know what the bottle says."

Taking the swaddled baby, he leaves the two of us alone in this filthy space. I grab a towel and a bottle of water.

"I don't know what I'm doing." My words are hard and tight in my throat.

"Neither do I."

I get her to stand, and I hold her steady as she wipes the blood and fluids between her legs as best as she can.

"Thank you for your help, Celia," she says. "I'm so sorry you had to do this."

I don't tell her she's welcome or that it's okay.

As far as I'm concerned, she's a sinner. A home-wrecker. The very kind of person my father would consider a harlot. My father betrayed my mother, but Alison betrayed me.

I trusted her.

I looked up to her.

I loved her like a sister.

"Here." I hand her four pain pills and a bottle of water.

"Shouldn't I feed the baby first?" she asks. "What does the book say?"

I hand her the textbook.

"I know you're upset." She goes straight for the table of contents. "You have every right to be. I know I messed up. No one's more disappointed in me than I already am with myself."

I say nothing because I have nothing to say to her.

What's done is done.

I have a new sister, my father is going straight to hell, and she's probably going with him.

My dad appears in the doorway, cradling the teeny infant in his arms. "We'll have you rest in the next room, Alison."

He nods toward the doorway across the hall, and we follow.

"She needs to nurse," he says, handing the baby back to Alison once we get her settled on the mattress.

I look away as she tugs the hem of her shirt up and the baby begins to fuss. A minute later, the fussing has stopped.

"Hungry little thing, isn't she?" my father asks, a hint of amusement in his tone.

Is he happy about this? Is this a joyful moment for him? If this were anyone else, he'd waste no time telling them they had just secured a one-way ticket straight to an eternity of damnation.

I step into the hall.

I'd walk home right now if I could.

I don't want to be here.

I don't want any part in this.

"You did a good job in there." He joins me a moment later, closing the door behind him. "I know that wasn't easy, but I'm proud of you for stepping in and doing what needed to be done."

Like I had a choice.

"She should've been taken to a hospital," I say.

He's silent. Either my words are ringing true or he's two seconds from backhanding me for my "smart" remark. Once again, the blow never comes. I suppose it makes sense, though—he isn't himself tonight.

He must be wearing another one of his masks.

"I tried to take her, Celia," he says. "I did. But she refused. She's been hiding this pregnancy from her family . . . If she'd have delivered at Cross Beach General or any hospital in a twenty-mile radius, it would've gotten back to her family before the kid even had a name."

"You mean *your* kid?" I might as well pile the comments on tonight, because for the first time in his life, my father doesn't have a leg to stand on. "What's going to happen when she shows up at home with the baby?"

"The baby's not going home with her," he says.

"Where's it going?"

"Home with us." He heads back into the room with Alison and the baby, ending the discussion and leaving a trail of unanswered questions behind him.

How is he going to explain this to my mother?

And will she be able to care for and nurture this baby?

Some days it seems like she barely loves Genevieve and me—will she have room in her heart for her husband's love child?

By the time he returns, Alison is out cold—I'm guessing thanks to the pain pills he stole from Mom's medicine cabinet.

"Your mother thinks I got called out for work," he says. "You need to keep it that way, you understand? She can't know about this. No one can. Or there'll be dire consequences for you, for me, for our entire family."

The steely flicker in his eyes tells me this is a promise, not a threat.

"Tomorrow morning, I'm going to go for a jog, and I'm going to say I found this abandoned baby in the park," he says. "We'll have to go through the right channels, a few formalities, but I'm going to petition that your mother and I adopt her."

It's sick, this plan.

"And Alison's okay with it?" I ask.

"It was her idea."

I glance toward the doorway, curious if he's telling the truth or if it's just another one of his onion-peel lies. I can't count how many times Alison's told us she wants to be a mom someday. Four children. A nice house with a big backyard. A red minivan with a DVD player for the kids. She had her whole life planned. While I'm angry with her for betraying us like this, a part of me is sad for her, too.

"This never happened, Celia," my father says with a frightening glint in his stormy blue irises. "Do we have an understanding?"

I swallow the lump in my throat before nodding.

I have half a mind to tell Alison to take the baby, run as far away from here as she can, and never look back.

CHAPTER 40

C ELIA

Present day

I've been staring at these flowers for at least an hour now, racking the fragments of my broken memory, assembling pieces together like a jigsaw puzzle. The uneasy feeling that has haunted me for the last two years—was it Celeste? Was she the one calling me? Was she the reason I felt watched everywhere I went?

And the note from the night of my party . . . June 14 was underlined twice and circled. It was never referring to my birth date—it had to have been referring to hers.

Ours.

I think of that morning weeks ago, when I sat in my car outside the train station, watched the woman in the car behind me flip down her visor, caught her following me into the ticketing booth area, and later on, saw her on the same train but in a different car.

Was that her?

Did she follow me into the city . . . and wait for the perfect chance to strike?

What does she know?

Was her intent to *kill* me?

And what will she do now that I'm still alive?

CHAPTER 41

CELIA

Present day

"I just remembered, I need to get some stamps," I tell Rob as we leave the grocery store. It's my first official outing since coming home two weeks ago, and while I had my reservations, I couldn't stand being cooped up in the house a minute longer. "Go ahead, I'll meet you back at the car."

"You sure?" he asks, pushing our cartful of groceries.

"Yeah, it'll just be a minute." I pull my ball cap down, ensuring my scar is still covered, as it can be quite jarring for people to see if they're not expecting it, and then I make my way to the customer service desk.

Two people are ahead of me, so I pull out my phone and tap out a few text message replies while I wait: First to Natalie, confirming that our travel insurance is covering the cancellation costs of our failed Tulum girls' trip. Then to Deirdre, rescheduling the hair appointment I missed while I was in the hospital. She claims she can do something with the jagged mop that is my postcraniotomy hair, but I told her we might as well shave it all off and start fresh.

"Next," the cashier calls when it's my turn.

I buy a book of stamps so I can send out thank-you cards from my party. My friends would be more than understanding if I neglected to send them at all, but I need something to keep my mind off everything else.

Before heading out to the parking lot, I stop into the ladies' room. Finishing up a moment later, I wash my hands and slick on a coat of pink lip balm before turning to leave. The door swings open as I reach for it, so I take a step back to stand clear.

"Pardon me," I say before realizing that I'm standing face-to-face with the woman who has haunted my every thought for the past twenty-six years. Only it's not Alison; it's her daughter.

My half sister.

I kept expecting something else to happen after she sent those flowers, but there were no phone calls. No eerie sense of being watched. No deliveries or cars creeping by at strange hours of the night. For a sliver of time, I breathed a little easier, thinking the worst was over. I rationalized that she needed to get something out of her system, to feel some sort of vindication, but for what I'm not sure. People hold on to all kinds of ideas about others, and I can imagine the stories she heard about me over the years didn't paint me in the best light.

"Hi, Celia," Celeste says with a terse voice that contradicts the unsettling smile on her face. "Got a minute?"

"My husband's actually waiting for me outside." I point to the door . . . the door she happens to be blocking.

"It'll only take a second."

"It's been you this entire time, hasn't it?" I take a step back. I may be farther from the exit, but I need to place some distance between us.

"My mother—my *real* mother's name was Alison," she says, ignoring my question. "I'd ask if you knew that, but I already know the answer."

I don't understand . . .

Did my father actually come clean?

He's much older now, closer to the end of his road. Impending mortality has a way of putting the fear of God into people and making them grow a conscience at zero hour.

Still, I don't buy it.

The Jim Fielding *I* grew up with wouldn't know what a conscience was if it hit him over the back of the head with a leather-bound Bible.

She takes a step closer, narrowing the careful distance I placed between us moments ago.

"Did you know she named me?" she asks, her head tilted just so as her piercing gaze pins me into place. "Celeste means 'heavenly.' Did you know that? Probably not. You've never really stopped to think about anyone other than yourself."

"I don't understand why you're doing this . . ."

"Really?" She chuffs, rolling her eyes. "He told me you'd do this . . . He told me you'd play dumb."

"What do you want from me, Celeste?" I hold my ground and ignore the way her menacing expression is the same one my father used to wear when he was about to throw me in the hell shack.

"I want to know *why*," she says. "Why did you do it?"

"Why did I do what?" My stomach drops as each second ticks by with agonizing anticipation.

The cruel anger in Celeste's eyes dissipates, replaced by glassy tears that she swipes away before they get the chance to roll down her freckled cheeks.

"Why did you kill my mother?" she asks.

Deafening silence lingers between us, disrupted only by the hammering of my heart inside my chest. I can only imagine the intricate web of lies my father has spun. This morning's breakfast sloshes in my unsettled stomach before rising up the back of my throat.

Before I can defend myself, the door swings open and two elderly ladies shuffle in, squeezing past us before disappearing behind neighboring stall doors.

"This isn't over," Celeste says under her breath. "Not even close."

With that, she's gone—before I have a chance to tell her the truth.

It won't be a matter of *if* I'll see her again, but when . . . and who knows what state of mind she'll be in next time—how worked up she'll be.

Her final words to me play on a loop in my head as I amble to the parking lot.

This isn't over.

She deserves the truth—only something tells me I may not get the chance to give it to her.

CHAPTER 42

GENEVIEVE

Present day

I lift my finger to silence my whining daughter the second Celia's name flashes across my phone screen. Charlie pouts—then again, she's been poutier than usual. She isn't used to having to share my time and attention with anyone, and lately all of it has been going to my sister.

This is a first for all of us.

"Celia," I answer. "What's going on?"

"Can you send me Celeste's number?" She's breathless . . . and this is another first.

Maybe she wants to thank her for the flowers she sent?

"Um, yeah. Of course. Is everything okay?" I ask.

Charlie's gaze flicks from her phone screen to me.

"I just saw her," Celia says. "I ran into her at the grocery store . . ."

I laugh because this must be a joke. "What are you talking about? Are you sure?"

She exhales. "Yes. It was her. We were . . . talking . . . and we were interrupted—and then she left."

"Wait." I switch my phone to my other ear. "Celeste is here? In Schofield?"

"That's what I said."

"That doesn't make any sense. She wouldn't come all the way here and not tell me," I say.

Celeste and I are close.

Unlike Celia and me.

The call goes silent, and I check to ensure she hasn't hung up.

"Do you remember when Celeste came into our family?" Celia asks.

"What kind of question is that? Of course I remember," I say. "Everyone called her the Cimarron Baby. Mom and Dad did that interview on the news after they adopted her. Why?"

She's quiet for a beat.

"I need you to call Celeste," she says. "And I want the both of you to come over as soon as possible. We have to talk."

CHAPTER 43

C ELIA

Present day

Rob squeezes my hand as we sit across from Celeste and Genevieve in our living room. Staring into the eyes of a woman who threatened me mere hours ago is nothing short of unnerving, but I need to clear the air . . . and my name.

At first, Rob was hesitant about infringing on our time, but I insisted he be here. Not only do I want to refrain from telling this story more than I have to, but I wanted the peace of mind of having someone bigger, stronger with me in case Celeste comes unhinged.

I clear my throat and glance at the untouched bottled waters resting on matching coasters on the coffee table that divides us. My palm sweats against my husband's, and heat prickles along the back of my neck.

"Thank you both for coming over on such short notice," I say. The formality of my words is strange given the deeply personal circumstances we're about to dive into. "I think there has been a misunderstanding." I clear my throat. "No, I'm sorry. It's not a misunderstanding . . . It's a lie."

Celeste squints. Or perhaps she's glaring. I don't know her or her nuances enough to tell the difference.

"Twenty-six years ago, on the night of my fourteenth birthday," I say as the words attempt to catch in my throat, "our father woke me up in the middle of the night, put me in his car, and drove me to an abandoned house across town."

My sisters haven't so much as blinked, sitting side by side like matching marble statues frozen in a moment.

"When I got there," I continue, "I found our babysitter . . . Alison . . . in labor." I release my hand from my husband's warm grasp and place it over my beating heart. "Dad handed me a textbook and some supplies . . . Everything happened so fast . . . but I delivered you, Celeste. It was terrifying, and it was confusing, and then there you were."

Genevieve's jaw is slack. Celeste looks down at her hands, her fingers knitting.

"Wait." Genevieve lifts her palm. While her voice is steady, her hand shakes. "Back up. I didn't know anything about this." She turns to Celeste. "You're Alison Lang's daughter?"

Celeste nods.

"You didn't know?" I ask.

Genevieve shakes her head, her attention passing from me to Celeste.

"She's Alison's daughter," I say with a careful cadence. "And she's our father's daughter, too."

Horror colors Gen's face for a moment, and then her eyes flash a stormy shade of blue. "Why didn't anyone tell me?"

"Dad made me promise not to say anything," Celeste says with a tremor in her voice as she wrings her hands. "But I didn't think it was right . . . that Celia did what she did and never had to suffer for it."

Gen sits forward, adjusting her posture as if she's uncomfortable. "What did you do, exactly, Celia?"

"She killed my mother," Celeste answers before I have a chance. Her gaze is pointed at me, and the shake that resided in her words a moment ago is gone.

Genevieve gasps. The weight of Rob's stare falls on me next. The two of them don't know what to say, sharing something in common for once.

"It isn't true," I tell them with the conviction of an innocent person on death row. "I was angry. I was angry with Dad. I was angry with Alison. I didn't know how to process any of it . . . When I confronted him, he told me that he and Mom were going to raise the baby, that it's what he and Alison wanted. End of conversation. He told me he was going to leave the baby in a park and then *discover* it"—I use air quotes—"while jogging in the morning."

Celeste's brows lift, and she crosses her arms tight across her chest. "Is this the part when you went back to the house and murdered my mother in a fit of rage?"

"No," I say, my voice a hair louder than I meant it to be. "This is the part where you have it all wrong, the part where our father orchestrated a heinous act—and got away with it for the last twenty-six years."

Genevieve's bottom lip quivers.

Celeste frowns.

"He had *everything* to lose," I say. "His career, his reputation, his legacy. Not to mention, your mother was seventeen. She was a minor. There was too much at stake if he let her take you and run away. If she ever came back, all it would take was a DNA test and a calendar and everyone would know what he did."

"You're lying." Celeste's expression hardens.

I maintain my composure, reminding myself she's been indoctrinated into Jim Fielding's warped view of the world.

"You have her eyes." Genevieve sucks in a startled breath before clamping her hand over her mouth. "Oh, my God, Celeste. You have her eyes. I . . . I always thought there was something familiar about them, and I remember now. The pale blue with the starbursts of gold . . . When did he tell you this? And why didn't you tell me?"

Celeste takes Gen's hand in hers, a tender yet heartbreaking move.

"Do you remember a couple of years ago, after Mom died, when Dad was in the hospital with chest pains?" Celeste asks.

Genevieve nods. "Yes, he ended up having a triple bypass."

"Right," Celeste says. "I'd stop by his room on my breaks and before and after my shifts, and the day of his surgery, he said he had a confession . . . that there was something he needed to get off his chest in case he didn't make it out of surgery alive. Of course, I told him he was being ridiculous, that he was going to be fine. But you know how he is . . . Anyway, that's when he told me about Alison. About his love for her. How she sang like an angel at church and treated his daughters like her own. He said she was the prettiest thing he'd ever seen, and while the last thing he wanted to do was hurt anyone, he gave in to his temptation—which led to me."

My stomach is in knots listening to a romanticized account of what happened, but I bite my tongue.

"Anyway, Dad said I deserved the truth," Celeste continues. "And that he was the only one who would ever give it to me straight."

"Or maybe he wanted to give you his version of events," I say. "On the off chance that he died in surgery and you eventually reconnected with me and learned the truth."

"I don't understand." Genevieve points between the two of us. "How does any of this mean that Celia killed Alison?"

"From what I was told, there was some jealousy and resentment at play . . . He loved me and he loved my mother, and Celia couldn't stand it, so she flew into a blind rage and stole my mother from this world."

The words she uses, the phrasing, all of it reeks of Jim Fielding.

Genevieve's lips twist at the side. "That doesn't sound like the Celia I remember."

"Thank you," I say before pursing my lips. I hope I don't come off too self-regarding, but I appreciate Genevieve's validation.

Rob rubs my shoulders, though they're still as tense as stone.

"You were just a kid," Celeste says. "How would you have known?"

"She wasn't a daddy's girl, I can tell you that much," Gen says. "In fact, she did anything she could to avoid being around him most of the time."

Celeste leans back on the sofa, her eyes unfocused on her untouched water bottle. I hope she's processing this, looking at it from another perspective. The fact that she has spent years believing I could've done something so heinous breaks my heart.

"And Celia loved Alison," Genevieve adds. "They were close—like sisters."

"If she didn't do anything, then why did she run away?" Celeste asks, gesturing with her hands before grabbing a fistful of her own hair.

I don't insert myself into their exchange. Despite the three of us being sisters, I'm on the outside of this conversation looking in. I may be the topic of this dialogue, but Gen's words hold more weight than mine ever could.

Genevieve almost chokes on her response. "Because that's what Celia always did—she was constantly running away. Things for her . . . They were different than they were for you and me."

There's a hint of pain in Gen's voice. Since we've been back in one another's lives, I've yet to address the way I left. I've always tastefully grazed past it and curtailed conversations before they veered into an uncomfortable territory. I always wanted to keep our exchanges light and happy, future focused—now I realize it was at the expense of the closure she badly needed.

"Dad always told me you left because looking at me reminded you too much of what you did to my mother," Celeste says to me, though her eyes don't meet mine. "He said that was why you didn't want anything to do with me."

I rest my elbows on my knees, bury my head in my hands, and drag in a long, cool breath before responding.

"Looking at you," I say, "didn't remind me of what I did . . . It reminded me of what he did. *What I saw him do.* I was fourteen, Celeste.

And I witnessed something no child should ever witness—after experiencing something no child should ever experience. I was traumatized."

Rob rubs circles into my back.

It isn't like him to be this silent, but I know my husband, and he's giving us this long-overdue moment and saving his own comments for later.

"One thing was always crystal clear," I say to Celeste. "He loved you more than I'd ever seen him love anything—other than God, his pastor, and his church. You were his sun and his moon. I'm glad you got the good parts of him because Genevieve and I? We didn't. I got the brunt of it. Gen was smart enough to blend in with the wallpaper most of the time. I was always running my mouth, asking questions, and getting myself in trouble."

"It's true," Genevieve says with a wince. "All of it."

"I swear to you, Celeste." I turn to my other sister and then my husband. "I swear to all of you, I didn't kill Alison. And I don't know how I can prove it because it's my word against his, and all the evidence is long gone. He made damn sure of that."

Jim Fielding is nothing if not strategic.

"He's had your ear the last twenty-six years, Celeste," I say, "and I get that you have no reason to believe me, that there isn't anything I can say that will convince you. But you heard his story . . . I wanted you to at least hear mine, too. I wanted you to know that I didn't kill Alison. He did."

CHAPTER 44

CELIA

Twenty-six years ago

The baby won't stop screaming, and Alison's out cold thanks to the pain pills my father had me give her earlier.

"You're rocking her too hard," he tells me. I don't think I am. In fact, I'm making an effort to be extra gentle. She's so tiny, smaller than a baby doll. I don't know if most newborns are this little or if she was born early.

He yanks her from my arms, and she whimpers for a few seconds before settling down.

"Should we wake up Alison to feed her?" I ask.

"No," he says, shooting me a stern look while he cradles her. "You let her rest, you understand?"

"When can I go home? Mom will be up in the next couple of hours. She'll know I'm not there, and if Genevieve—"

"Just go find a place to sit down and be quiet. I can't think with all of this fussing coming at me from every direction." He bounces her in his arms, harder than before, and he returns to the room where Alison is resting.

I step over empty beer cans and fast-food wrappers, over cigarette butts and stained carpet, and peek through the blinds of the living room window before finally giving in and taking a seat on the ripped sofa. Closing my eyes, I try not to think about the filth around me. And for a lack of anything better to do, I count the seconds to pass the time.

One . . . two . . . three . . . all the way to eight hundred twenty-seven.

I take a break from counting and decide to trek down the hall and check on Alison and the baby. The door is cracked a few inches, and I peek inside to spot my father kneeling at her bedside, his head down as if he's praying.

Typical Jim Fielding.

Alison appears to be sleeping, the baby swaddled against her chest. But after a minute or so, her arm turns limp.

My father tilts his head up, snapping off a pair of gloves.

Confused, I watch as he places a syringe on the floor beside the mattress before taking the baby from her arms.

In a flash, it becomes crystal clear.

"What did you do to her?" I ask, swallowing the scream threatening to leave my throat. "*Dad.* What did you *do*?"

He turns around, unhurried, unstartled, and wears a frighteningly calm expression.

"Don't work yourself up, Celia. I just gave her a little something for the pain," he says. "Take the baby while I finish up here. We're leaving soon."

"Finish up? Finish *what*?"

He doesn't answer; he simply places the baby in my arms before motioning for me to leave the room.

But I don't leave.

I place the baby gently on the floor before rushing to Alison's side. She's still warm, she's still breathing, but her breaths are slow and staggered.

"What did you inject her with?" I ask.

"I told you to take the baby in the next room and wait."

I push past him, shaking her shoulders in an attempt to get her to wake up.

"Alison," I say, lowering my lips to her ear. "Alison, wake up. Please. You have to wake up."

My father hooks his hand under my arm, pulling me away, but I grab on to her shirt, scrambling to get out of his clutches.

"*Alison,*" I say between sobs. My vision is blurred with tears, and everything around me is muddled darkness. "Wake up, please. Please, *please* wake up . . ."

With a firm jerk, my father pulls me off her and directs me toward the door.

"Go wait in the car." He tosses his keys at me. They land at my feet. "Or *else.*"

I don't remember walking to the car, but all of a sudden I'm there.

I sit in the back seat, passenger side, as far away from his seat as possible.

None of this feels real.

Closing my eyes, I pray to a God who may or may not be listening, and I ask him to make all this a nightmare.

I'm pulled from my prayer when my father returns. He opens my door and places the baby on my lap before he climbs in front. The engine roars to life. The sky around us turns yellow, orange, and pink at the horizon.

We stop at a park on the way home, and he leaves the baby in a covered piece of playground equipment.

"You ever speak a word of any of this to anyone and it'll be the last thing you ever say. I'll make sure of that," he says once he's back in the car. If he's capable of hurting an innocent woman to cover up his own sin, he's capable of anything.

"You killed her." Tears stream down my cheeks, but I'm too exhausted to wipe them away. "What happened to 'thou shall not kill'?"

"That woman," he says, a disgusted sneer on his lips, "that . . . that *Jezebel* . . . she seduced me, she led me astray. She brought out a side of me that never should've seen the light of day."

I think about the last time Alison babysat us and she was telling us about her newest boyfriend. It seemed like every time she came over, she had a new one. But I'd never seen her eyes so lit or her cheeks so flushed as they were this time. She was breathless almost, and I remember telling her love looked good on her. She told us he was tall and handsome and brave. The way she spoke about him made me think of a fairy-tale prince. He sounded dreamy and perfect, like he was her own personal knight in shining armor.

"Every action has a consequence, Celia," he says. "If you take anything from all of this, let it be that."

"How can you justify killing someone?" I sob the second the words escape my mouth.

"That's between me and God," he says without an ounce of emotion, like he's speaking straight facts.

I think of the pain pills. He wasn't trying to make her comfortable—he was trying to knock her out so he could euthanize her like some hopeless, injured animal.

He had a plan all along.

My chest burns when I think of Alison dying on that dirty mattress in that horrid house.

Maybe she made a mistake, but she didn't deserve to die for it.

My father's eyes are strained and focused as he grips the steering wheel at a perfect ten and two on the drive home.

I used to think there was nothing scarier than Jim Fielding.

But now I know I was wrong.

The scariest thing on earth is a man who plays the very same God he claims to worship.

CHAPTER 45

GENEVIEVE

Present day

Celeste is taking a breather on the back patio while Rob comforts Celia in their kitchen. I camp out in the living room, numb and shell-shocked, replaying the pieces of our conversation on a loop in my mind.

"You believe me, don't you?" Celia asks when she returns.

Rob is in the kitchen, standing there, staring out the window above the sink like he's lost in thought. He's been her person for the past twenty-two years, and I imagine he's just as blindsided as the rest of us.

"I do," I say to her. "It makes sense to me—your story. Knowing the kind of man he is, the kind of man he was always pretending to be . . . Celeste doesn't know that version of him."

"Good for her," Celia says with a wry sniff. "And I mean that. Good for her."

"You were a different version of yourself after Celeste came into our lives, too," I say. "I always thought you were maybe a little jealous of the new baby. Then I thought it was because we were always the ones taking care of her, feeding her, changing her, putting her to bed. So I started taking over most of those things, thinking it would cheer you up. But it never did."

Celia offers a pained smile as she listens.

"Then I blamed it on your hormones. You were getting older. And you were moodier. It all went hand in hand," I say. "When you ran away your freshman year of college, that was tough. But I wasn't surprised. And I never blamed you. But it hurt. It was like losing a piece of me I knew I'd never get back."

Celia moves from her sofa to mine, though she doesn't put her arms around me or rest her head on my shoulder—not that I expect her to. I was always the touchy-feely one of the two of us.

I think of the letter Rob shoved in my face that day—the one he accused me of writing. And then I think about Isabel's comment about Celia feeling watched. Lastly, I think of the attack in the city, the one that nearly robbed her of her life. My heart shatters at the thought of Celeste being behind all those. I don't want to believe it's true, but at the same time, it's the only thing that makes sense.

That eye-for-an-eye mentality wasn't the only thing passed on from our father to his youngest daughter.

It's terrifying the things we'll do in the name of those we love—and in the name of those who love us.

Someday soon, we'll sort everything out. Until then, we'll process one thing at a time—together. I'm hopeful that with a little time and a lot of forgiveness, the three of us will be closer than ever.

Rob may be a tougher sell, but I've witnessed how much he loves Celia. I imagine there isn't much he wouldn't do to make her happy, especially after almost losing her forever.

"Celeste doesn't know what to think right now," I say. "There's got to be a way we can convince her."

Speaking of, our youngest sister returns from the patio. I move to the side and open up a place for her to sit in between us. Even if she isn't 100 percent sold on Celia's account of things, she needs to know we're all in this together.

"You said it was the night of your fourteenth birthday?" I ask Celia when we're all together again.

"Mm-hmm," she says.

"Oh, my God." I stand before pacing the space in front of the fireplace. "That night I woke up with a bad dream in the middle of the night. I tiptoed to your room—like I always did—only you weren't there. Your bed was empty. I checked the kitchen next, but you weren't there either. I was getting myself a glass of water at the sink when I saw two headlights pull into the driveway . . . That's when I saw you and Dad getting out of the car."

I stop walking and cup my hands over my nose and mouth.

"It's true. I remember now. The night Celeste was born, Dad and Celia were gone . . ." I say as my hazy memories become clearer by the second. "And Celia was different after that. Like a shell of herself. I never understood why . . . and now . . ."

My words trail into nothing before I collapse on the sofa, exhaling as tears rain down my face. Celeste doesn't hesitate to wrap her arms around me tight. She buries her head against my shoulder. A moment later, the couch cushion on my other side sinks, and a second set of arms slips around me. Warmth blankets my body, and my tears turn dry.

The three of us sit in silence for an endless moment before it hits me.

"Does Dad know you're here?" I ask Celeste.

"No," she says. "Why?"

"I have an idea," I say. "Celia, would you be willing to make a phone call?"

CHAPTER 46

CELIA

Twenty-six years ago

"Celia." My father's voice lures me from a hard sleep in the middle of the night, but I don't move. Instead, I pray I'm dreaming. I keep my eyes shut tight, hoping I'll fall back asleep, that the sound of his voice and the heaviness of his presence will fade back into the darkness where they came from. "Celia, wake up."

He gives my cheeks a gentle smack with the back of his hand, not hard enough to hurt but enough to force my eyes open.

"Get dressed." He tosses a pair of my tennis shoes on the floor. "We have an errand to run."

My alarm clock reads 2:46 AM.

I shove my foot into one shoe, biting my tongue to keep from asking if I'll be delivering another one of his babies tonight.

As soon as I get the other shoe on, he hooks his hand under my arm and leads me out the back door to his car. I rub the sleep from my eyes and stare out the window. The world is crystal clear this time of night, all the stars shining brighter than they did the night Alison had her baby.

I don't know where the baby is now. After my father "found" her at the park, he handed her over to social services. I just hope wherever she is, her caretakers love her the way Alison would have.

My father turns down an unfamiliar street, then another, and another, but soon the houses we pass begin to look familiar.

We're going back to the crack house . . .

My stomach drops, and a million words are stuck in my throat.

He pulls up to the street in front of the abandoned house from the other night and motions for me to follow him in. This time we go in through the back door. One step inside and the pungent-ripe tang of decay smacks me in the face. The house reeks ten times worse than it did the first time. I pull my pajama top over my mouth and nose and follow my father's tall silhouette through the messy hallway and to the last bedroom at the end.

"I need your help cleaning this mess up," he says. When he steps out of the way, I'm met with Alison's lifeless body. Even in the darkness, I can tell the color has vanished from her pretty face. Her eyes, which were once sparkly and as blue as the sky over the Atlantic, are wide open, staring at the ceiling above, and her mouth is agape.

My insides heave, and I brace myself on the wall, fighting off the urge to lose the contents of my stomach.

"It's just a body, Celia," he says. It's easy for him to say. Working in public safety his whole life, he's seen more dead bodies than he can count.

At fourteen, I've never even been to a funeral.

"You grab her legs, and I'll get her upper body." He moves toward her head, hooking his arms under her stiff torso.

I stand paralyzed, unable to move, unable to breathe, unable to process all this.

"Come on, now. Don't just stand there," he says.

"I don't want to do this." I don't care what punishment he fits me with this time. I'm drawing the line here.

"You don't have a choice," he says without pause, his expression twisting.

"Why did you bring me here?" Alison's not very big. Maybe a few inches taller than me, is all. Whatever he intends on doing with her, he easily could've done himself.

"Grab her feet, Celia."

"Not until you answer me." This is the most I've ever challenged my father in my whole life. I fully expect a beating of some kind when we get home or a couple of days in the hell shack. But I don't care. This is insane, and I want no part of it.

"Because if there's blood on my hands, there needs to be blood on your hands, too."

I squint. "I don't understand."

"We're in this together, whether you like that or not. You helped birth that baby. You saw the necessary measures I had to take that night," he says. "We're going to dump her body in the canal behind the house. The gators will take it from there."

"So you're destroying evidence . . ." My words trail off. "I thought you were trying to make it look like she overdosed?"

"It'd only be a matter of time before someone found her here," he says. "And after the autopsy, they'd be able to tell she'd just given birth—and how long ago that was. It would coincide with the abandoned baby in the park . . ." He waves his hand. "I don't need to explain any of this to you. Just know that if I go down for this, I'm taking you with me."

"So you're blackmailing me?"

"I'm glad you can read between the lines, Celia. Now grab her feet so we can get on with this." He hoists her upper body off the bed. *"Now."*

"No."

Dad lets go of Alison, and her stiff, bloated body falls onto the mattress like a rock landing in mud. Before I can process what's happening, he's flying across the room, his hand wrapped around my neck.

He shoves me against the filthy wall, pinning me with his weight, his face so close to mine I can smell his sour breath.

"I brought you into this world, and I sure as hell can take you out of it." His voice is a low growl forced through gritted teeth. "Challenge me again, Celia. See what happens."

His grip tightens against my neck, all but crushing my windpipe. I couldn't speak if I wanted to.

He gives me one more wild-eyed look—an unspoken threat—before releasing me.

I gasp for air, my throat on fire with each breath-reclaiming cough.

Without saying another word, I help my father haul Alison's body to the canal, and then I help him clean up the bloody sheets and any evidence that any of us were there that night.

CHAPTER 47

C ELIA

Present day

"Hello?" My father's voice on the other end of the line sends a shock through my middle, despite the fact that I'm the one calling him. I never thought I'd have to hear his voice again, not in this lifetime.

I've been dreading this call for two days, working up the nerve and preparing my questions.

Strategizing the way he would.

"It's Celia." I hold the phone flat on my palm, the microphone close to my lips in hopes he won't realize he's on speakerphone. Rob, Celeste, and Genevieve are gathered around me, holding their breath, silent as church mice. Genevieve is recording the call, though I'm not sure why. We would never be able to use it as evidence in a legal case, as it's illegal to record conversations without consent in Florida. Maybe she wants it as proof for her own sake—or for Celeste's.

The other end is so quiet, I have to check and make sure he didn't hang up. But the call timer is still going. He's there; he's just silent.

"What do you want?" he asks as if I'm a bothersome telemarketer burning a hole in his afternoon.

"I need to talk to you about something."

"Unless you want to talk about how you ruined your life and undid all the hard work your mother and I put into raising you, then there's nothing to talk about."

Twenty-two years haven't changed him an ounce.

"I actually wanted to talk to you about my fourteenth birthday," I say.

I'm met with dead air, and once again I check to make sure he's still there.

He is.

"Celia, I'm seventy-two years old. I can't tell you what I ate for breakfast this morning, let alone reminisce about one of your birthdays."

"I bet you'd remember this one if you tried," I say. "I'm happy to help you if you need."

The cat must have his tongue again.

"You woke me up in the middle of the night . . . had me put my shoes on . . . drove me to an abandoned house . . . forced me to deliver your teenage mistress's baby . . ."

"I don't recall any of that," he says, choosing his words carefully. "Must've been a dream."

"More like a living nightmare," I say. "I remember everything about that night. Crystal clear. Even the address of the house: seventy-two Palm Avenue. I saw the house was condemned a few years ago and the city tore it down, but is that canal still there?"

"Celia, now I know you didn't call me just to shoot the breeze about some canal."

"You're right. You're absolutely right. I think you know exactly why I'm calling."

"I'm afraid you'll have to be more specific than that," he says.

"All right. Fine. I'll spell it out for you. Alison Lang was pregnant with your baby; you stole the baby, killed Alison, and dumped her body in the canal behind that crack house. Need me to keep going?"

"Jim, who's on the phone?" an unfamiliar woman's voice asks from the background. That must be the replacement Mrs. Fielding.

"No one, sweetheart," he says, his tone as soft and sweet as cotton candy. "It's just a sales call."

"Then hang up on them," she tells him.

"It'll be just a minute," he says. "Go on outside, I'll meet you on the patio in just a bit."

The smooth slick of a sliding glass door follows; open, then shut.

"Doesn't seem very *godly* of you to lie to your wife," I say. "Is there a reason you don't want her to hear this conversation?"

"Listen here." His voice is a low growl. "Don't you *ever* call this number again, do you understand? I don't know what you *think* you remember, but you need to forget it. Now. It never happened."

"Did you ever ask God to forgive you for killing an innocent woman?" I ask.

"Innocent? That *Jezebel*? That woman was nothing but—" His words stop short, as if he realizes he's slipping. It isn't a confession, but it's close. I blame his old age . . . and his God-sized ego.

"Ah, so you *do* remember her."

"Vaguely," he lies. "I remember she was never up to any good."

"Your memory is foggy, yes, I know," I say. "You've made that abundantly clear with the whole not-remembering-what-you-had-for-breakfast thing."

"I'm not going to sit here and tolerate your mockery."

"That's fine. I mean, you brought me into this world, the least I can do is show you a little respect, right? A little courtesy? That's why I wanted to give you a heads-up."

"About what?"

"About the thorough murder investigation being launched." I'm bluffing, of course.

He releases a smug sniff of a laugh. "That's cute. Real cute. Good luck with that."

"Oh, I don't need luck."

"If I go down, I'm taking you with me." The audacious confidence in his mocking tone is insulting, but I don't take it personally. He's not going down without a fight and some good old-fashioned denial, but I don't let it scare me.

I'm not fourteen anymore.

He'll never put the fear of God into me again.

There's nothing he can hold over me, nothing he can say, and now, there's nothing he can do to stop the maelstrom of justice we're about to rain over him.

When I sat down with my sisters two days ago, we went over everything we knew in great detail, piecing the puzzle together with scraps of memories until we had a timeline. With my testimony and Genevieve corroborating the fact that we were both gone the night of my fourteenth birthday, we're hopeful it's enough to launch an investigation. And if it isn't, then at least we'll have something none of us had before . . . closure.

"Good luck with that," I tell him, using his words from a moment ago.

I end the call, and the four of us collectively exhale.

"You okay?" Genevieve rubs Celeste's back.

Celeste's gaze is forward and unfocused, and I'm not sure if she's quite processed everything yet. Our dad was her hero. He was her person. He could do no wrong in her eyes. This can't be an easy pill to swallow.

"It's a lot to take in all at once." Celeste's voice cracks. "He called her a *Jezebel* . . ."

I wince.

"He told me she was the love of his life," she adds. "And with you he wrote her off like she was nothing . . . And the tone of his voice . . . so smug, so evil . . . It was like you were speaking to someone else. That isn't the dad I know."

"He's a master manipulator," I say. "I'm sorry you had to see that side of him."

Genevieve hands her a tissue before a single tear has a chance to fall. Gen was always so nurturing with her, and I'm thankful that hasn't changed over all these years.

"What about you?" I ask Gen. "Are you okay?"

Her attention passes from me to Celeste and back. Gen was never a daddy's girl, but she never experienced his wrath the way that I did. I imagine she's holding an entire mixed bag of emotions about all this.

Rob squeezes my hand before leaning close. "I'm going to leave the three of you be."

I move to Celeste's other side. I want her to know I'm here for her, that I hold nothing against her. She was fed a mountain of lies by the one person she trusted. Her hatred of me was indoctrinated.

Celeste's delicate body folds in half as she buries her head in her hands. It's in this moment that I think of something Rob told me when we first started dating: hurt people *hurt* people. I didn't understand it at the time. I thought he was implying that hurt people have a right to hurt others, but that wasn't what he was saying at all.

I place my arm around her shoulders and rest my cheek against her arm. The baby I delivered twenty-six years ago is now a full-grown woman who's lost everything she's ever cared about.

At the end of the day, we're both victims of our father.

We're in this together.

Every person he's ever come into contact with has been a victim of his evil ways.

His gaslighting. His manipulations. His conniving. His lies.

"He's not going to get away with what he did to her," I say. "What he did to *us*. I promise, Celeste. He's never going to hurt anyone else, ever again."

EPILOGUE

CELIA

One year later

"Happy birthday, Celia." Rob clinks his champagne flute against mine.

"To Celia," my closest friends chant, lifting their glasses.

I begged Rob not to throw me a do-over celebration (his words, not mine) this year, but he refused to take no for an answer. It's a smaller party—same faces, less fanfare. A strict no-gift policy, which he surprisingly enforced this time.

"Celia, you're radiant as ever tonight," my hairdresser says between sips. "I'm so glad we went bold with your hair. Loving the pixie cut on you. It really brings out your cheekbones."

"I know Rob said no gifts"—my good friend Natalie saunters up to me, her phone in hand—"but it's on my phone, so it technically doesn't count, right?"

"What'd you do?" I ask with a chuckle.

"I rebooked our girls' trip," she says, showing me an email of our new itinerary. "I'll forward it to you."

"Can't wait," I say, before turning to Neal and Deanna. "Thank you so much for coming tonight."

Deanna kisses the air beside my left cheek. A few months ago, she found out her lymphoma is in remission. That very night we all dropped what we were doing and went out for dinner to celebrate. Deanna's been spending her days celebrating every little thing, ever since. Literally. She says she intends to live the rest of her life as if it's one big, long, never-ending celebration.

"Hey, there." I mosey up to Gen. She's currently planted at the cake setup with my sixteen-year-old niece, who's only here to act as her parents' designated driver—and only because they're paying her. Genevieve said it's their way of teaching her responsibility, selflessness, and entrepreneurship. I don't pretend to know a thing about parenting. It's not a road I ever wanted to go down after the experiences I had, but watching my sister be a better mother than the one we had fills my heart with a special sort of tenderness.

We broke the chain.

"Hello, hello, sorry I'm late." Margaux Mansfield enters in a cloud of perfume, waving at everyone from across the room before making a beeline my way. "Happy birthday, gorgeous. Love the hair, love the dress, love your whole vibe tonight. Forty-one looks good on you."

"Thank you," I chuckle.

"I didn't bring a gift because your old ball and chain said we couldn't, but I think you should know that bag you had your eye on is on sale right now. Thirty percent off," she says, leaning in. "Should you choose to buy yourself that bag tomorrow, consider that savings to be my gift. You're welcome."

She trots across the room to chat with Holly, and I take a moment to breathe. To take this all in. To appreciate the ones I love and the ones who love me back. I've learned in my forty-one years that there's no such thing as having too many friends. That the people who aren't meant to stay in your life inevitably fade into the background sooner or later, and the ones who are meant to be there will find a way to you one way or another.

"Just think, we would've missed all of this had I taken that job in Kansas City." Rob sidles up to me, giving me a nudge. "I'm so glad you talked some sense into me."

"You needed a change of pace, not a change of scenery." Once the dust settled last year, we had a heart-to-heart about his sudden urge to change jobs. It turned out the hospital in Kansas City was half the size of the one he was running in Schofield. We determined he was burned out, that he needed a sabbatical and a new job with a little less weight of the world on his shoulders. After a six-month mini-retirement, he landed a job managing a small network of local urgent care centers.

So far, so good.

On the other side of the room stands Celeste—my youngest sister. In the year that has passed, we've gone to therapy together and spent countless nights alongside Genevieve, talking until the sun comes up and reclaiming the sisterhood we never had a chance to have.

Everything that happened these last several decades is officially water under the bridge.

Our lives—each of them—begin now.

"Hey," I say when I make my way over. "Love the dress—where'd you get it?"

She winks. "A little boutique here in town . . . you may have heard of it? It's called Celia's Closet."

I swat the air before leaning in to give her a hug. "Thanks for coming."

"I wouldn't have missed this for the world," she says. "Happy birthday."

"Happy birthday to you, too."

After the case against my father was assembled, he was charged with first-degree murder and statutory rape. Unfortunately, the statute of limitations prohibited them from also charging him with obstruction of justice, evidence tampering, and abuse of a corpse. Once a DNA test confirmed he was Celeste's biological father, Genevieve's testimony about seeing us arrive back home the night Celeste was born helped seal the case.

Once Alison's parents were alerted about the investigation, they were able to provide old diaries where Alison wrote about her affair with my father, referring to him only as "John." After knowing the connection and combing through her writings, it was easier to pinpoint exactly to whom she was referring. Of course, it wasn't enough to submit as evidence in his trial, but it was enough to rectify any last shreds of doubt Celeste was battling.

After attempting—and failing—to pin the crime on me, our father pled not guilty. And is currently appealing with the help of a church-sponsored legal team. But he doesn't stand a chance. He'll spend the remainder of his days behind bars, wallowing in the pitiful sea of his own denial.

"Wondered where the birthday girls were hiding." Rob saunters over to us, pulling me into his warm leather- and vetiver-scented hug. It's the very same embrace I fell in love with twenty-three years ago this summer. I press my ear against his chest, listening to the steady drum of his heart, and he kisses the top of my head. "Happy birthday, Celia. And to you as well, Celeste."

From this birthday forward, I'm going to ensure June 14 will be celebrated the way Alison would have wanted.

May she finally rest in peace.

ACKNOWLEDGMENTS

Heartfelt thank-yous to Jessica Tribble Wells, Charlotte Herscher, and the entire Thomas & Mercer team. Your behind-the-scenes magic is second to none, and you are all such a dream to work with. *Gone Again* marks our sixth book together. Here's to many more!

To my agent, Jill Marsal—thank you for your savvy advice and for believing in me from the start.

To my husband, thank you for your continued support as I follow my heart—and for always holding the fort down when I hole up in a hotel for the weekend for some uninterrupted writing sessions.

To all the readers, reviewers, bloggers, Bookstagrammers, and BookTokers . . . I couldn't do any of this without you. Thank you, thank you, thank you.

Last, but not least, this book is dedicated to our dog, Milo, whom we said goodbye to during the editing of this story. I will forever miss his soft snores and his warmth at my feet. He was a constant companion, always by my side as I wrote morning, noon, or night. Thank you, Milo, for fifteen years of unconditional love. Until we meet again.

ABOUT THE AUTHOR

Photo © 2017 Jill Austin Photography

Minka Kent is the *Washington Post* and *Wall Street Journal* bestselling author of *The Watcher Girl*, *When I Was You*, *The Stillwater Girls*, *The Thinnest Air*, *The Perfect Roommate*, *The Memory Watcher*, and *Unmissing*. She is a graduate of Iowa State University and resides in Iowa with her husband and three children. For more information, visit www.minkakent.com.

Made in United States
North Haven, CT
18 October 2024

59104253R00143